MOON MAYOR

CHRIS MEEKINGS

Copyright © 2022 Chris Meekings
Copyright © 2022 Hybrid Sequence Media
Cover Artwork © 2022 Kristen Tomaru
Cover Design © 2022 Donald Armfield

All rights reserved. No part of this publication may be reproduced, distributed, or transmitted in any form or by any means, including photocopying, recording, or other electronic or mechanical methods, without prior written permission of the publisher. Permitted by copyright law.
This is a work of fiction. Names, characters, businesses, places, events and incidents are either the products of the author's imagination or used in a fictitious manner. Any resemblance to actual persons, living or dead, or actual events is purely coincidental.

ISBN: 9798418887320

Massachusetts – Gloucestershire

0021

Constitution Alternations

Amendment 1	1
Amendment 2	7
Amendment 3	15
Amendment 4	22
Amendment 5	27
Amendment 6	32
Amendment 7	37
Amendment Pixie	42
Amendment 8	49
Amendment 9	56
Amendment 10	62
Amendment 11	66
Amendment 12	71
Amendment 13	77
Amendment 14	83
Amendment 15	87
Amendment 16	94
Amendment 17	102
Amendment 18	107
Epilogue	113

moon mayor

Chris Meekings

Amendment 1

The Judicial power of the Gyre shall not be construed to extend to any suit in law or equity, commenced or prosecuted against one of the Gyre by Citizens or Subjects of any Foreign State or Planet. Citizens are advised that Foreign Planets or Citizens of Foreign Planets do not exist and therefore cannot hold legal sway, or cause death.

An oceanic breeze caught onto myriad discarded sweet wrappers, making them crinkle and rustle. Smells of toffee and liquorice swirled with the wind and tossed them at a couple. The couple sat together on the old rust-colored tugboat's bow surrounded by garbage. The water splashed and crashed over the creaking vessel's hull and echoed through the shiver-timbered wharf creating its own screeching noises.

The couple sat at the helm of Marcus' old, beat-up, rust bucket of a tugboat, which was tied to the rickety wharf of one of the outer islands of the Gyre.

Caroline moved her hand, lovingly over Marcus' face. Her fingers traced the beautiful scars and stitches, crisscrossing over his face as if they were etched by the starlight.

A semi-repaired CD player, kicked out Hooty Blowhard's "I Wanna Frisk You, Baby." Pieces of electrical tape wrapped around it, barely held the batteries in place. Marcus had made the mix CD for Caroline, containing all her favorites. Every song got her in the mood. Although Marcus well, he got her in the mood less so, at least when he talked. Caroline was sure she was going to have to dump him soon enough. Even here, on the tiny Gyre, she'd be able to find a better boyfriend.

The surrounding night was alive with stars, twinkling and twitching on the velvet black sky. The moon was nowhere to be seen, which was odd because it should have been, considering the clear sky. Caroline didn't think about it, the moon just wasn't there. Blue, glowing pixies moved above on the garbage landscape, shouting obscenities, and making crude gestures at the couple. The flotsam garbage accumulated below their boat, fusing with the already heaping garbage mass.

The Gyre was a mass of swirling human detritus caught in the ocean's eddies. Thrown together by greed and want in equal measure; it was also the place that Caroline called home. The compacted garbage over the land was nothing but a solid pile of stink and growth, which was what all life did. And people had come, in the end, and made a home of it. Caroline's home. "Beautiful night," she said, trying to go through the motions.

Marcus nodded.

The lug really couldn't hold much of a conversation, but he was honest, and a good mechanic, Caroline thought. The rust bucket of a boat only stayed at float because Marcus was good at salvaging and cannibalizing parts he collected. He wasn't bad looking either, well, for a greaser. He had black hair, slicked-back, and he wore a cool leather jacket with inlaid studs. And then there were the scars, those delicious stitched-up scars. Maybe she wouldn't dump him, not just yet.

Marcus dug his fingernail into a stitch on his forehead, opening the wound. It bled. Blood trickled down his face in scarlet rivulets, covering every inch of his face. The blood steamed over the night air.

Caroline leaned in. She ran her tongue over Marcus's cheek, the rasp stubbles of hair pricked at her tongue. His blood filled her mouth, and she swallowed every bit. The taste was so good, like old blackberry wine.

"Come on," Marcus said, "Let's get away from the sea. Someone might come by. We'll go into the woods."

He jumped to the wharf and motioned for Caroline to follow.

Caroline giggled and jumped to her feet. She was definitely in the mood.

Marcus took her hand and led her to the dark forest.

Pine trees stood tall, over the heaps of rubbish, now fused with what use to be the ground. Trees which had grown from cones, and floated to the Gyre only to take root, and grow over the rubbish, like ancient pilgrims making their new life. Needles crunched under Caroline's shoes, as branches clawed her face. Marcus turned and gave her a broad smile.

The pines tress looked dark and forbidding, practically growing into one another, not allowing much starlight to shine through. The scent of pinesap and Caroline's chewing gum mingled with the dense clouds above.

Glowing pixies sat on some of the higher branches with long fishing rods trying to catch fireflies.

"Fuckers! Fuckers! Fuckers!" taunted one. It stuck its fingers in its mouth, pulled its cheeks apart and crossed its eyes.

"Give her a proper seeing for me!" shouted another pixie, thrusting its hips.

Marcus and Caroline ignored the crude fair-folk. Pixies were always rude to everyone. The only way to calm them would be to smear jelly on their noses, but there were far too many in the forest to attempt that.

The lovers entered a clear patch, except for the pine tree that had fallen a week before. The trees were totally bare of fairy-folk, although Caroline could still hear them up in the trees behind them. Above the stars still twinkled in the sky. There was still no moon, and Caroline continued to ignore the situation. "It's so beautiful," she said, staring up.

"Not as much as you," said Marcus, which wasn't the worst line he'd ever tried.

He grabbed a handful of her hair and placed it between his lips. He sucked. Caroline felt shivers down her spine. It was an electric tingle, which she always felt when Marcus nibbled her hair and slurped her sweat. She nuzzled his neck and bit into it, feeling his blood pulse and spurt down the length of his chest. She loved the taste of his flesh.

    An agonizingly bright light from above scorched the ground around them. A giant beam of bluish-white brilliance; engulfed the whole clearing. Caroline shielded her eyes, trying to see what caused the glare. It must be a helicopter or something like that, she thought, but she couldn't hear the sound, the whoomp, whoomp, whoomping of the rotor blades—which really should have alarmed her.

    Silently floating above was a gigantic, disc-shaped craft. Bright lights sporadically bursting out from the edges of hovering disc. A vast beam of light shone from beneath its center, like a search-beam and still no sound. The odd ship just eerily hung there in the sky. The pixies fell silent and so did the forest.

    Deathly still.

    Static electricity bursts over Caroline's arms, biting at her skin. Transfixed by the light, as it skewered her with its radiance. Caroline was unable to move. A gust of wind swept through the clearing, pine needles nipped and stung her ankles. "What...what is it?" she somehow managed to ask.

    Marcus just stood there slack-jawed and wondering, as the harsh lighting cast monstrous shadows over his face. The wind thrashed upwards, throwing his hair back from his forehead.

    The light intensified, Caroline could feel her skin heat up, as the light continued to course through her. She squeezed her eyes shut, tears had begun to fall and roll down her cheeks.

    ...And then the heat dissipated. She opened one eye to peek if the light had died out as well. Marcus and herself were no longer alone.

    Two six-foot-tall, spindly figures with large bulbous heads and black almond-shaped eyes stood before them. The figures were both completely naked, but also totally sexless, in comparison to human parts. Caroline surprisingly was not alarmed, yet hesitant to move.

The two spindly entities approached; more of flowed, rather than walked, it was as if they were superimposed into the landscape. Their faces were totally expressionless, but Caroline could smell the menace coming off them.

She backed away, her fear finally overcoming her paralysis. She tugged on Marcus' sleeve, trying to get him to follow her. But the big lug was rooted to the spot, enthralled by the advancing beings. Caroline's heart raced in her chest, like a trapped bird in a cage. She wanted out.

She wanted away from these things.

She wanted to run, and she wanted Marcus to run with her. Back to the boat. Away!

Anywhere!

"Come on, let's go!" she said, panic pulling her voice tighter.

Marcus stood stock still, sweat beading on his face. His eyes were wide, glassy and staring, but he did not budge. Caroline let go of his arm and backed away.

The spindly beings reached for Marcus. The leading figure stretched out one of its long-fingered hands and ran a curved digit down one side of Marcus' face. It tilted its head to one side, curiously, as if it were trying to figure out what he was. The being turned its head, taking one look at Caroline before dismissing her and returning to Marcus. Its opalescent eyes transfixing his stare even deeper into nothing.

The being reached behind its back and brandished a metal tube. Marcus screamed; a deep guttural-wrenching sound as if his heart was tearing through his chest, his veins pulsing through his skin, almost thrumming to its own rhythmic sound.

Caroline screamed in terror as his skin went black and cracked, exposing fissures of blinding yellow light. She stumbled backwards, tripping over a tree root and landing on her rump.

Marcus was lifted into the air by some unseen force, connected to the beam of light. His screams were louder, more frantic as the light erupted from his blackened skin. One final flash of light and he exploded into tiny particles of dust.

Caroline awoke, sprawled out on the ground. A pixie was kicking her ear. "Oi-you, Fuck-face! Get up!" it said, kicking her again. Caroline rolled onto her belly and hesitated to stand. The pixie scampered off.

Why was she on the ground in the forest? Caroline tried to recall her whereabouts.

She got up, unsteadily, coughing and spitting a thick wad of phlegm on the littered ground. A hard frost had settled over her body, and she shivered.

There was a leather jacket strewn over a pile of dust on the ground at the forest's clearing. Caroline moved hastily to the jacket, thinking warmth. She noticed a name: '*Marcus*' written on the inside label. She didn't know who that was, but she was grateful he'd left his jacket behind.

Confused about how she'd gotten to the forest, she walked the distance back to shore. Floating by the ocean's edge was an old, rust-colored tugboat. Clambering aboard and steeling into the wheelhouse, she discovered that the keys were in the ignition.

Lucky her.

When she turned the engine over music began blasting out of the speakers. It was Hooty Blowhard's "I Wanna Frisk You, Baby." She turned the song off. She'd always liked the track, but it was a make-out song. One day, she hoped, a guy might make a mix CD for her and add that track to its contents. That one guy would be a boyfriend, ultimately the future.

Caroline piloted the tug back into town. She would keep the tugboat and the leather jacket. And no one will question where she got them from.

Amendment 2

In all criminal prosecutions, the accused shall enjoy the right to a speedy and public trial, by an impartial jury, consisting of real things only, and to be informed of the nature and cause of the accusation; to be confronted with the witnesses against them, to be confronted by the psychics who predicted it, to be dressed appropriately in a manner befitting their station, to have compulsory process for appropriating witnesses in their favor, and to have the Assistance of Counsel for their defense—also a shoelace monitor to make sure they don't trip over.

Abraham Lincoln, Mayor of the Gyre, had no relation to the famous Abraham Lincoln, the 16th President of the United States—absolutely none. That was the first thing he always wanted people to know, he was not related to 'that' Abraham Lincoln. Yes, he was a politician. Yes, he was married to a woman named Mary. No, he did not have a chin-strap beard, and no, he did not wear a stove-pipe hat. And, as a further follow-up, yes, he thought the emancipation of the slaves was a beautiful and excellent thing. He was a totally different guy. Happy now?

Abe sat at the dining table in his rather elegant and lavish mayoral house, his head buried in the newspaper as he reread the offending article. He tried to think of a way out of the impending shitstorm that was no doubt coming his way, both domestically and professionally, no obvious one occurred.
The headline was pretty bad, it read: *Honest Abe Caught with Headless Beauty Queen.* It could have been worse. It could have been a zingy-pun, something people would remember, maybe: *Lincoln Rides,* or *Happy Birthday, Mr.*

Mayor. As it was stated, the article was bland and factual, and maybe, forgettable?

However, the accompanying picture was very, very bad indeed. Lurid even, and he had no doubt it would stay with the voters.

The picture next to the article showed Abe sprawled across a putrid motel bed with a bloody shocked look, smeared across his face, and his thin, pigeon-chest on display. The sexy, erstwhile headless beauty queen vixen, sat on his crotch. With her back to the camera, unmistakably in the throes of ecstasy. Her nipples had been tastefully covered with stars. Abe's nipples had not, which he felt was pretty sexist.

"Lies! It's a whole pack of lies, Mary. Fucking vultures, printing this trash," he lied.

He reached over and grabbed his coffee mug, embossed with the words "World's Greatest Mayor." This was another lie he told himself just so he could sleep at night. He took a deep draught of the hot, bitter liquid. The future always looked better with hot coffee in his belly, especially the free-range Kopi Luwak coffee, which he had imported for his exclusive personal consumption.

"That is some damn fine coffee, Mary," said Abe.

There was no reply.

Abe glanced around the room, but there was no sign of his wife. He got up from the table and searched the house, but still couldn't find her.

Mary was gone.

This situation should have alarmed him. Instead, a cool, calm collective thought crept over him, as he repeated the words to himself. *"Mary was gone?"*

It felt like a misty haze was covering his memories, as they all seemed to fade away.

Mary?
Mary?
Mary who?

He pulled out his wallet and took out a photograph of himself and some young woman he didn't recognize.

Why was he keeping this?

Well, she was pretty, but he didn't really remember the woman. He scrunched it up and threw the photograph in a garbage bin. Then he took a ring off his finger and dropped it into a container he kept an assortment of half-working pens.

He returned to his cup of coffee and took a sip, now noticeably cold. The newspaper still spread opened accusingly on the table taunted him. The photograph of his own flash-paled face staring back at him. Abe slammed his fist down onto the table. Why had he been so stupid? The memory of the headless vixen flashed through his memories. Ah, yes, that had been why he had been so stupid: her incredible body, those full ripe breasts, that delicious neck stump. He licked his lips at the thought of her. What was her name? Amber? Annabelle? He could barely recall the contest he had been asked to judge where he had seen her name on the badge that dangled around her neck. All he could remember was the beautiful stump, and the way she tasted. The way he ran his tongue over her sweet, sweet esophagus, as it flapped over and parted. He shook his head vigorously, trying to clear the thought—there was no time for that.

A barrage of chatter outside drew his attention to the window. Slowly, he pushed the curtain to one side and peaked out. A maelstrom of reporters and photographers were corralled in the front garden, and there were more on the boondocks at the garden's end, and even more perched on tugboats floating in the street.

Carrion feeders, he thought to himself. *Journalists, come to pick my corpse clean.*

An envelope, he tossed aside earlier, still sat accusingly unopened on the dining table. Abe really didn't want to open it. He did not want to read its contents. Perhaps if he ignored it, it would all go away, but that wasn't how the world worked. You couldn't just ignore things and therefore make them disappear.

The future was before him, and he would just have to embrace it, for good or ill.

He slit the white envelope open with a thin letter opener and replaced the blade in his jacket pocket. He pulled out the crisp folded letter. It read as expected:

"The council had met late last night. They thanked him for his service as Mayor, especially his recent judging of the Miss Headless Beauty Pageant and his continued championing of the new ice-cream parlor's plans. However, in light of his behavior, bringing the Mayoral office into disrepute, his term as Mayor was under consideration. He was summoned to the Council Chambers immediately, where his further duties would be decided."

That was ominous. It was tantamount to a firing, in only a few hours. Abe bit his lower lip as he tried to think of his options. He could refuse to turn himself in, which would lead to him being dethroned as mayor. He could run away to the sea and become a sailor, but that seemed impractical, and although like every Gyre citizen, he could sail a boat, he really wasn't an ocean-going man. He could turn himself in, which would probably lead to him still being removed from office, but at least with dignity, and maybe, just maybe, he could talk his way out of it. Talking his way out of situations was pretty much his bread and butter. Turning himself in was probably the best option. It offered a tiny glimmer of hope.

There was a knock at the window. Abe raised the kitchen blinds revealing a young, willowy woman standing outside the window. Her dyed-blonde hair was pulled back in an austere scrapped ponytail, and her thin face was adorned by a set of black-rimmed glasses. Abe was pretty sure someone had told her that it would make her look professional, but they actually made her look distinctly inexperienced.

"Mr. Lincoln! Mr. Lincoln!" she yelled brightly from the other side of the window.

Abe opened the window, which was a huge mistake. Before any of the others came asking questions at his window, Abe said, "I have no statement to make at this time." He was about to shut the window when one of the woman's well-heeled shoes got in the way. The shoe was followed by a shapely ankle and a delightfully long leg. That flustered him more than it really should, he was still half thinking of Amber? ...Annabelle? ...Alison? the headless woman.

The intruder pulled herself through the window and stood up in the sink. Her shapely ankles submerged beneath the waterline, which strangely was not emptied and contained two plates even though Abe lived alone. Or did he? The young woman tried a disarming smile, which ended up looking psychotic. "This will only take a moment of your time," she said and pulled out an owl from her jacket pocket.

She lifted the bird to cover one of her eyes and squeezed it. The owl hooted, and its eyes exploded into light and smoke. Abraham was startled, coughing, and waving the pall of thick, grey smoke. The woman removed the spent eyes of the owl and screwed two new ones in, that miraculously appeared in her hands. The owl spat out a black-and-white photograph of Abe after giving a brief hum. The picture was unflattering. The woman took out a pencil and notepad and started to jot things down.

"And before you ask, I'm no relation, what-so-ever," said Abe, cutting off the usual question and trying to find a footing in this unwelcome conversation.

"Very well, Mr. Lincoln," the woman said, keeping eye contact with Abe as she scribbled in her notepad.

"My name is Caroline Brooks, reporter for The Daily Nihilist. I wish to do a feature on you, and, of course, cover this recent incident; get your side of the story, so to speak? My first question is, what does your wife think about all of this? My readers would love know," the reporter asked.

"I'm not married," said Abe.

The reporter looked blankly at the sink she stood in; two dishes slightly floating in the water, two coffee mugs resting on the table across from her and the two chairs positioned at the table. Her eyes returned to the mayor.

"Of course, you aren't," she said, scribbling a few more things into her notepad. "Abraham Lincoln, mayor, bachelor," she said aloud.

This damn reporter crawled through his window, he wished there was a more often occurrence, but young woman usually didn't' climb through his window.

"Young lady, this interview is not possible at the time. I am going to have to ask you to leave. I am in no fit state, or able to address anyone. I have a meeting today with the council, where we shall go about our normal daily duties and discuss several upcoming projects; like the plans for the new Ice Cream Parlor District's construction."

The reporter furiously scribbled more notes.

"Stop writing things down! I told you, I would not do an interview today," he said, leaning over to read her notes, curiously wondering if she spelt his name correctly.

"You're going to the council chambers? Excellent, I'll join you. We can do the interview after," she said, putting her notebook and pencil away. "We should take my boat; it's moored out in the back. That way, we can avoid the others," she indicated the front door where the ravaging pack of journalists stood on the other side.

Abe eyed his front door. He imagined shadows looming behind the door; dark, hulking shadows of many, journalists ready to toss him to the wolves, wanting a their own scoop. A string of bad headlines began to develop inside his head. Credible accusations and indictments unfolded in imagined ink. He turned his gaze back to the young reporter.

She was just one woman. She couldn't be more than a few weeks out of college. A young cub-reporter. A young and dumb, cub-reporter...

12

Yes, that might do. He could mold his own story, twist things.

Indeed.

He could see it now: "*Put Upon the Mayor's Story*", "*How I Was Set Up*", '"*I Thought It Was Love, How Wrong I Was*" "*Abe's Confession.*" This could possibly bolster his poll ratings; sympathy votes were always worth mining.

"Alright," he sniffed, "you're on. I'll allow an exclusive interview, on the understanding that I get to see it and approve it before you print it. And, I think you're right about the front door; we'll take your boat to the city council meeting."

"Agreed on the interview," said the reporter. Obviously, she was delighted to get the scoop she wanted. "Do you have a plan about what you're going to say to the council?" she asked.

"We're just having a normal meeting," he lied.

The reporter raised an eyebrow.

Abe made a mental note that the reporter was not as gullible as she looked.

Abe hadn't thought ahead to plan for what he would say. He just needed the willpower to force the council to not fire him, an angle to sway the members and pluck on their heartstrings. Or he could try bullying them? They will not take him down; he was the god-damn Mayor!

"I'll make an impassioned speech about the freedoms of man, and man's inalienable right to love whomever he chooses. And, if that doesn't work, by God, I'll call them all prudes!" Abe stated.

Caroline Brooks gave him a slightly worried look, shook her head in bemusement and spun around in the sink and climbed out of the window. Abe took a faltering step, somewhat concerned that he hadn't even managed to convince her, then clambered in tow behind her.

The gathered crowd's noises around the front of his house were deafening. Surreptitiously, Abe peered around the corner of his house to inspect the townsfolk's wrath.

The crowd was large, ill-mannered and belligerent; some had pitchforks, and a few had actual burning brands. Journalists were scattered among the group, some with notepaper and pencil, some with audio recording weasels, and a few had high-powered photography eagles. Everyone was making judgmental statements, inciting hate speech, or shooting the breeze about last night's local football game.

Someone had lynched his milkman from the old apple tree in the front garden. Abe suddenly realized why there hadn't been any milk delivered that morning. The elderly milkman swung lazily from a hemp rope, his eyes bulging and bloodshot. Abe shook his head with pity. He thought about the milkman's prompt deliveries; rain, storm, low-tide or high-tide, he was indeed a great milkman.

Quietly, he and Caroline made their way to the her boat.

Amendment 3

The right of citizens to vote shall not be denied or abridged, curtailed or made a bloody nuisance by the Gyre on account of sex, gender, being a girl or being of the womanly persuasion. Seriously, sexism is not cool.

Caroline scampered across the dock, launching herself onto the deck of her boat. She landed catlike and made straight for the wheelhouse as Abe carefully climbed onto the rocking ship.

The reporter's ship was an old, rust colored tugboat. The beat-up hulk had grown a bumper crop of baby-heads in its nooks and crannies, and the pungent aroma of rotting flesh, dripping with blood wafted in the air. Abe wrinkled his nose at the scent.

"Is this vessel river worthy?" he coughed, holding his nose against the vile smell.

Caroline turned and glared at him. "Of course, it is," she barked back.

"It doesn't look river worthy," said Abe, totally missing the glare. "Do you even know how to drive this thing?"

Caroline bit back the idea of calling him a sexist pig.

"You can walk if you want, but..." She guided her voice between her hands in the direction of the reporters corralled at the front door of the mayor's house, "Mr. Lincoln, Would you mind answering some questions, please? Mr. Lincoln! Mr. Lincoln!" Her voice got louder with each word. Abe quacked in protest, but it was too late. Checkmate.

A vast of reporters came around the building at a dead run with their eyes set soulless and wild. They raised high-powered telescopic eagles and pelicans. There were flashes and screams of pain; as the roiling mass of humans ran toward the dock.

15

Abe's eyes widened, and he flustered with his footing, debating which way to turn.

"Shut up and hang on," Caroline yelled.

She gunned the engine and sped away. The reporters tumbled into the river, like lemmings. They bobbed unhappily in the dank water, jostled by detritus and garbage as the chop broke over them.

Abe and Caroline sped down the river highway at a relatively quick pace. Caroline was damned if she wasn't going to drive fast. And she was double-damned if she'd let Mayor Abraham Lincoln affect her speed in any way, what-so-ever. The stuck-up, misogynistic prig.

Above them flying saucers crisscrossed the sky. Some of the saucers hovered in one place over the river, other saucers freely flew around the sky. One of the saucers took an interest in Caroline's boat. It stopped directly overhead and beamed a bright yellow light down over her boat. Caroline and Abe steadfastly ignored it. UFOs did not exist. Therefore, that couldn't be a UFO. The baby-heads, growing in the crannies, cried in alarm as the beam passed from bow to stern and back.

Eventually, the UFO finished its scan. Having found nothing of interest, it zipped away in a flash of light. Caroline and Abe both sighed and then remembered that they should ignore UFOs as they didn't exist. Nothing had happened because nothing like that could have happened. There was nothing to remember, the last few seconds were of no interest. A blur.

Caroline accelerated down the garbage-strewn waterways of the Gyre. The water was slick with ooze and the generally acquired flotsam that eventually accreted into the Gyre. Plastic coffee cups, Styrofoam, cardboard, fishing lines, fizzy drinking bottles and the rest of humanity's detritus all slowly coalesced together to form the islands that they called home. It wouldn't take long to get to where the city council meeting was taking place.

Caroline cut the engine and let the boat slide up to the quay before mooring it firmly. They ascended the giant Romanesque-steps, carved from the very garbage landscape itself, to the Council Chambers.

The Council Chamber's lobby was crowded with lawyers and lawmakers, clerks, velociraptors, and other city officials bustling about; shuffling papers, or pouring over extensive ice cream menus. Crabs scuttled about the patrons' feet, picking up scraps of garbage, and using them to repair walls.

There was an audible hush which descended on the room as people recognized Abe. To his credit, the mayor straightened himself and strode straight past the gawping onlookers.

The room the council always held their meetings in, was the farthest in the building. The idea was to intimidate people coming to complain by making them walk past all the officials as they approached with their essential businesses. This was only partially successful, as still some citizens worked up enough ire to attempt to see the council. The labyrinthine corridors usually exacted their toll of those remaining troublemakers. There were rumors of entire "lost complainer" tribes who now lived in some of the less frequented halls, feeding on unwary clerks and stray crabs. So, when all was said and done, hardly anybody ever saw the council when it was in session.

When Caroline and the Mayor arrived at the door, Abe straightened his bowtie and pulled his shirt taught across his lithe frame. Then, he kicked open the doors to the council meeting room.

The room was large, with luxurious oak-paneled furniture finished in scarlet leather. A twinkling candelabra lit the room, wax dripping down the gold-leaf exteriors. The carpet was lush and vibrant red yet squished underfoot from the rising damp moister in the air, leading to a horrible scent throughout the government building.

The council sat on a raised dais at the end of a long walkway. All the members jumped as Abe kicked the door open and strode in, his face a storm cloud of determination.

There were four members to the council, two men, one woman and a hedgehog. The first man was short and squat with bowed shoulders and a distinct stoop. Around his neck, on a leather halter, was a giant rock. The word *Budget* was engraved on it in deep dark fissures.

The second man was long and thin. His cheekbones were sharply chiseled, his hair dark and swept back. The scars which ran across his forehead were lush and wept a sensuous ooze of milky fluid and blood. Caroline felt her heart flutter at the sight of the scars, but she righted herself quickly, *foolish, biological nonsense*. The man wore a white, oil-stained T-shirt with the logo *Committee Member for Commitment* written on it.

The council's female member wore dark spectacles on her round face. Her hair was frizzed in a static ball, probably meant to look like a perm. In front of her sat a bowlful of gravel, which she unconsciously dipped her hand into and munched on. She wore a deep purple sash across her midriff, which bore the legend *Spokeswoman for Internal Wants*.

The hedgehog was a hedgehog; small, spiked, pointy-nosed mammal. It shuffled happily on the table with a neat cardboard sign in front of it saying, *Social Justice Hedgehog*. It snuffled at some of the papers, rubbing its head over the ink. It stared at Abe and Caroline with beady, piercingly intelligent eyes.

"Social Justice?" squeaked the hedgehog.

"The hedgehog makes a good point. Do you have anything to say in your defense?" said The Spokeswoman for Internal Wants. Unconsciously she grabbed another handful of gravel and ate it; blood leaked out of her mouth and dribbled down her chin, broken teeth piled up on the table below her.

Abraham grabbed his lapels. He shuffled in place and stuck his chest out and began to address the council.

"Four scores and seven hours ago, this great city's mayoral office was brought into disrepute by yours truly. I was engaged in an act of lustful, carnal knowledge, and this I cannot deny, nor should I deny, for she was a woman, and I a mayor. But, my friends, is it not said by Herodotus himself: 'Ego participant in quis est coniunctio maris et feminae?' So, who among you can cast the first stone; or leading lady in the new play at the theatre opening tonight?

In undertaking your essential tasks, it is all together both fitting and proper that you, as esteemed council members, should bring forth wrath and vengeance upon my head, I see that now. It will be a great testing of my resolve, so conceited, seeing whether it can withstand the anger of the betrayal that I have thrust upon this illustrious assembly, with my dalliance and romances. But, speaking of the romance languages, always remember Pinocchio is spelt P, I, N, O, double C, H, I, O.; and I knew that before it was famous."

Caroline had no idea what he was talking about. Why did he insist on making such a speech that said nothing? Surely, he must realize pontificating made him an ass.

She stopped listening as Abe waffled in deep rhetorical nonsense. She wrote the word *bored*, over, and over, and over again in her notebook. After half a page, she tried to write it in Arabic. 'ana 'asheur bialmulil.

The shadows in the council meeting room flickered and loomed over the candlelight. A breeze wafted through the chamber, bringing with it the waterway's aroma; horrid, thick, and clawing.

"But in a larger sense we cannot, nor should not, belittle what I have done, in the penalty box, when the referee wasn't looking," continued Abe. "The world will little note, nor care, nor write on the words I say here today. But they will think on and fustigate with your decision. No statues will be torn down, nor should they be, even if they reflect poorly on today's thought processes, for they are our history, which we never learn from. In judging this headless beauty contest, I performed my tasks as Mayor without fear or favor and in fact, I judged her tremendously beautiful. It was a perfect encounter."

Abe had worked himself up. Steam rose from his ears, and his face was gammon red.

"As you go perilously into that goodnight and vote on my fate, cry havoc, to the bonds and oaths to which you swear—nay my friends. Cry havoc, and be with me, a leader among tortoises!"

He finished, throwing his hands into the air to deafening applause which only he could hear.

Caroline finished making notes about Abe's speech. She reread what she'd written only to find she'd misspelt *windbag*, *noxious* and *pompously*. Never mind, she'd sort that out on the proof-read.

The four council members looked puzzled.

"Abe, you great ass," said The Council Member for Budgetary Responsibility, the heavy weight of office pulling his head down almost to touch the table. "We voted on this an hour ago. It was only prudent and responsible to move quickly. You've been replaced."

Shock bleached Abe's face.

"Replaced? What the fuck? But you can't! All my years of service? All the plans we have for the future! The ice cream parlor. You can't replace me! I am these fucking islands!" shouted Abraham Lincoln, spit flying from his lips.

Ah, there he is, thought Caroline. She scribbled some notes. *That's Abraham Lincoln.*

"Social Justice!" squeaked the hedgehog, bouncing up and down in excitement.

"That's quite right, hedgehog," said the Committee Member for Commitment, "we've committed to have a new mayor."

"A new mayor? Already?" asked Abe with a snarl. "Surely, there needs to be some kind of vote from the electorate?"

"Social Justice!" squeaked the hedgehog.

"Abe," said The Spokeswoman for Internal Wants, "I want to introduce someone who we've all longed for and wanted for ages. Our new mayor, The Moon."

The councilwoman raised her hand. Caroline furiously made notes.

From behind a curtain The Moon stepped out to stand before the people. The glowing, pale, silver moon stood nervously on the raised dais as all four council members applauded. It bowed solemnly and then beamed at them in contentment. It rolled to the council's head seat and placed itself in the plush leather chair.

Amendment 4

A well-regulated menagerie, being necessary to the security of a free State, the right of the people to keep an armed bear, shall not be infringed.

The barber's shop was empty. The barber's shop was nearly always empty these days. People's hair still grew, but the islanders tended to cut their own as a money-saving scheme, because the unemployment rate was so high, at least that was what Michael Chandler believed as he swept the last hairs into a small pile. He got down on his hands and knees, and, reaching for the cut hair, stuffed a handful into his mouth. He chewed, tasting the brunette and blonde hairs.

A UFO descended over the street. It hovered low in the shop's window. Michael ignored it—things like UFOs didn't exist.

The immense size of the spaceship filled the window, only being obscured by the sign which read: "*No dogs, no dinos, no dead.*" The craft was a sleek, shiny-grey metallic saucer. The bottom section rotated at a blistering pace and small twinkling lights dotted out the top of the saucer. The swooshing wind, caused by the UFO, made the seawater outside chop and billow.

A search beam probed over the shop's front window. It illuminated the inside with a painful, bright white light. Michael squinted, but continued to ignore the thing, mainly because it couldn't really be there.

The light ran up and down the shop, but having found nothing of interest it flickered off into the sky. Michael sighed, then remembered that UFOs could not exist, so he shouldn't be sighing in relief. Nothing had happened, because nothing could have happened. *It is of no interest*, he thought and forgot about the UFO.

The floor was now nice and clean from hairs. Gently, Michael leaned forward and licked the black-and-white tiles. "Yes, they are spotless," he said.

He heard the doorbell ding as a customer entered his shop. Michael turned, seeing who it was.

"Ah, Mrs. Freeload, how nice to see you. And you've brought the bear in for his monthly trim," said Michael, smiling.

Mrs. Freeload stood in the doorway wearing her customary dress made from sewn together pages of Dickens' novels. Martin Chuzzelwit and Bleak House blew lazily in the breeze brought in from the street. Her hair was a flame red, molded into the shape of a scooped ice cream cone. This was done to add to her height as she was a very short woman. In her hand, she held the leash of her pet black bear.

The bear was probably the most depressed animal Michael had ever encountered. Its fur was black as coal and well-groomed. On its head, it wore a disgusting pink bow, which Mrs. Freeload replaced every day because the bear would mysteriously "lose" it overnight. Its collar was also pink. Its red-rimmed eyes stared into Michael's soul, pleading for him to shoot it and put it out of its misery.

The bear reared on its hind legs and moved its paws and signed in language, "Existence is nothing, but empty pain screamed into an uncaring void cosmos."

Michael imagined a future in which he had the guts to pull out a shotgun and finish the poor creature off, but times were hard, and although he didn't serve animals, Mrs. Freeload was an important and, more crucially, a paying customer. The woman always ignored the bear's signing. Michael wasn't even sure if she knew the bear was smart enough to sign.

Mrs. Freeload snapped the leash, and the bear dropped to all fours and trundled forward. It huffed, and slobber dribbled from its snout. It awkwardly clambered up into the barber's chair, which was about six sizes too small for it, and balanced as dutifully as it could.

Michael grabbed the clippers and started to shave the bear. The hair fell to the floor in a beautiful waterfall of inky blackness, and the shop filled with the stink of bear musk, to which Michael wrinkled his nose.

"So, Mrs. Freeload, are you and your husband keeping well?" asked Michael, as his clippers shaved the bear down to its pink skin, revealing the tattoos beneath the fur.

"Oh yes, the council work keeps him busy. It's a very responsible job being the Council Member for Budgetary Responsibility. It takes up most of his time. And, looking after my wonderful Bobo takes up most of my time," said Mrs. Freeload, making a fuss of her bear.

The bear grunted in surrender at the treatment. Michael was sure he saw an actual tear roll from its eye and get soaked up in its fur. He ignored its plight and continued to shave the bear bald, revealing the satanic tattoos on its goose-pricked flesh.

"Who's a good boy? Who's a good boy?" cooed Mrs. Freeload.

The bear looked at Michael dolefully. It signed, "I and everyone I will ever know will eventually crumble into dust, and our consciousness will go into the black embrace of death."

Behind him, reflected in the mirror, Michael saw a shimmering light. He and Mrs. Freeload turned, gawping at the flickering space. A gust of wind whipped through the shop, causing the pages of Mrs. Freeload's dress to rustle.

The bear, still in the throes of despair, signed, "I am just a speck in an uncaring hurricane of atoms and energy all travelling towards a cold entropic end."

Two spindly figures materialized from the shimmering light. Both were tall with bulbous heads and pitch-black, almond-shaped eyes. The creatures were pale grey in color, and both were totally naked as they stood there in the shop across from Michael and Mrs. Freeload.

The spindly figures turned their heads quizzically at the pair of humans who stood transfixed and open-mouthed.

"Ummmm...errrr....hello?" stammered Michael. "Did you two..." he paused and looked at the sexless entities, "fellas want a hair-cut?"

The pair of entities did not say anything. They were hairless and did not need a haircut.

"Look, you two...things," said Michael, angry that he wasn't going to make a sale. "You can't come barging into my shop being hairless. And, don't think I'm being racist here. I don't allow bald men in either."

"I don't like them, Michael," said Mrs. Freeload. The pages of her dress swished to Oliver Twist and Barnaby Rudge. "They are upsetting my bear. Throw them out, at once!"

The bear signed, "Existence is pointless and fleeting. Why should I care if anyone is happy or sad? Why do you care if I am happy or sad?"

Michael took a step towards the entities. The leading creature raised its gaunt hand, and Michael felt his body stop; his muscles seized. There was a great tearing pain in his chest. He couldn't breathe. His feet left the ground, and he was suspended in mid-air.

Mrs. Freeload screamed, as the other entity reached behind its back and pulled out a metal tube, pointing it at her. Her scream increased in pitch and volume as black fissures raced across her skin, like hyperextended veins. They conjoined until her entire skin turned black. Her skin began to crack and bright yellow lights emanated out of the cracks in her body. Her tongue thickened, and her eyes filled with blood. The pages of her Dickensian dress charred, Great Expectations and The Old Curiosity Shop crisped to ashes. Mrs. Freeload burst into a shower of dust and fell in a neat pile on the floor.

The two entities turned their heads to inspect Michael. He whimpered. Cracking slits broke across the faces of the beings in a rough parody of mouths. The slits opened wider, revealing greasy, pink-flesh maws. They let out an awful scream, of a high-pitched sound, and blood began to run out of Michael's ears.

One of the entities pointed the metal tube at him, and Michael felt a burst of hot energy erupt inside his stomach. His skin felt too tight as if it were contracting. His vision clouded to a milky white blur as the fluid in his eyes boiled. The immense heat crisped Michael's skin and it began to flake and fall to the floor. Within in seconds, Michael died. His remains fell to the floor into a pile of dust.

"Pain and sorrow are as fleeting as laughter and joy. One day, all will turn to fire as the sun expands, our once lush planet will burn and be consumed by our sun. That itself will burn out and vomit our atoms into the cold, dead wasteland of the empty universe," signed the bear.

The two spindly beings looked at the half-shaved bear and its satanic tattoos. The bear glared back. The entities dematerialized, just as they had when they entered the shop. The bear didn't care. In the end, everything was pointless.

Amendment 5

The sale of services to wash, or transportation to a place of washing, or public washing of laundry within the Gyre is hereby prohibited. (Repealed in 1922)

Everything washed up on the Gyre. Eventually. From the simplest wheel to the most complicated computer, they all sloshed up on the shores of the Gyre. If a thing was broken and thrown away, then it wound up accreting here. And the residents scavenged through the remains, repaired them and used them for what they were.

The Gyre was a dump, a pile, a heaping everything, flotsam and jetsam, the lost and the broken. All was swashed together and dragged along by the tides of the sea and then resurfaced onto the land.

And every idea washed up on the Gyre's shores too. But, generally, only the bad ones, as the good ones never got thrown away. It was a repository of every crummy idea and thought, every could-have-been, every never-was, every ought-to-have-been. They all ended up at the Gyre too. A never-ending cornucopia of patchwork detritus and theories and every kind of person to go with it.

The owner of the launderette watched Abraham Lincoln walk back and forth with his hands clutched behind his back in rage over his suspension from being mayor. The goat and owner of the launderette at two and a half feet tall by three and a half feet long, and a penchant for eating anyone's woolen socks if the washer's door were left open. Mr. Horns owned the only launderette in Gyre: *"Mr. Horns All Night Launderette."*

Mr. Horns wandered up the center aisle between the spinning washers as they tumbled and whizzed through their various cycles. Occasionally, he checked to see if any machines had finished and if their doors happened to prop open. He did this for reasons which were certainly "not to look for woolen socks."

In front of Mr. Horns, Abe continued to strut up and down the tiled-linoleum floor, clucking and talking to himself.

"It's not right, not right at all," he tutted.

Caroline, sitting nearby on one an orange plastic seats, was busily engaged in recording his thoughts and adventures for her exclusive piece in her newspaper. The young woman had given up on trying to write all the complexities and nuances of his journey and was now trying to capture it in a monumental, abstract painting.

"I have to admit; I did not expect that," said Abe, addressing Caroline, but not stopping in his pacing. "The Moon? Who gets replaced by The Moon? It's embarrassing. I'll take him down. We need dirt on The Moon. Real dirt. Something we can use. It cannot be allowed to govern. I won't stand for it. I'm sure it is unconstitutional or against the rules!"

Caroline drew a triangle in one corner of her painting, coloring it green. Abe glanced over at her painting, while pacing the launderette and was unsure what the green triangle represented in the whole abstract piece, but he was sure a green triangle must be a noble thing.

"How is it against the rules?" Caroline asked, pleasantly

Abe stopped pacing. How was it against the rules? He pondered for a moment, searching for a law which The Moon must have broken.

"I don't believe The Moon is a citizen of the Gyre, it's certainly never paid any taxes. Therefore, it cannot hold office!" he said, raising a finger to the heavens. "It's obvious. AND, we are going to prove it. That is the very reason we are in this launderette. Do you not pay attention to anything I do?"

"How is being in a launderette got anything to do with the Moon's tax status?" she asked.

Abe stopped pacing. Looking concerned he asked, "You really are very young, aren't you?"

Caroline picked up her brush and painted a red, slash across the green triangle.

Mr. Horns butted past the ex-mayor, having ascertained that Abe's washer was neither finished nor did it contain any socks. Mr. Horns made a goaty mental note that the device was full of papers, which were sometimes good for chewing on.

Abe went back to pacing and thinking to himself, waiting for his machine to finish its cycle. What was that bastard lunar-body doing? Its place was in the sky. Why was it down here? Why this city? Why was it interested in being mayor? Abe felt it was after something, but what? He needed answers, luckily that's exactly what the launderette was for.

The washing machine cranked up to a full cycle. The documents spun inside, sloshing down with purifying, soapy water. Abe stood in rapt attention following the sluicing documents.

"It's raining," stated Caroline, as she painted in a blue square.

Abe glanced over at Caroline's painting again. *"Did the blue square possibly represent the rain outside?"* Abe wasn't sure, abstract impressionism had never been much of an interest to him. The future was what brought him interests. Abe the future of these great islands! And his own political future.

He squatted down to watch the washing cycle go into draining mode. The papers tumbled and dropped to the drum's bottom as the soapy water burbled away. Nearly ready. It would be in there, within those documents. He could almost taste it. The papers would bring the downfall of The Moon and with its defeat would come his chance at reinstatement. He hummed an upbeat marching tune. He was about to fire the first shot in a war. A war with The Moon.

With a clunk, the washing machine finished, and the door opened. Abe grabbed at the paperwork inside, which was steamy and sodden, and it burned his hands. He began reading the soddened documents, devouring every word on the pages:

Moon, age: Unknown.
Moon, weight: Unknown, (it's very rude to ask.)
Moon, birthplace: Unknown.
Moon, citizenship status: Pending.
Moon, voting registration: None on record (probably a leftie).
Moon, favorite tea: Lap-Sang Souchong.
Moon, color: Grey (brown on closer examination).
Moon, preferred position: Splayed Lotus.
Moon, first person to walk on surface: Neil Armstrong.
Moon, status of dark side: Unknown –
(Radio contact lost with all Apollo Missions upon circumnavigation of Moon, astronauts will not speak of it upon their return.)

Well, that was maddeningly unhelpful. He re-scanned it. So, The Moon might be a leftie – bastard lefties and their bleeding hearts. And it had a dark side, well there was a possibility in that, something to exploit at least. If only he could identify something illegal, it had done. The Moon's birthplace was unknown, so it couldn't be a registered citizen. His instincts were right, the Moon was a foreigner. It was probably here under false papers or something. The Moon was an illegal immigrant, no doubt about it.

A grin split his face, and his eyes lit up like diamonds in a coal mine.

There was a ding as the door to the launderette opened. Abe ignored it. Civilians coming to do their washing were unimportant. What was important was he'd found what he was looking for.

A shiver ran down his spine as the temperature in the launderette dropped. Abe, again, ignored it as temperatures were unimportant. All that was important was the Gyre's future, the future of his premiership as Mayor Lincoln.

"Here it is, Ms. Brooks, my road back to the top!" he sneered.

There was a crunching thump as if something frozen had hit something hard. Abe heard Caroline exclaim and slump to the floor. An icy-cold, wet hand gripped his shoulder. The fingers dug deep into his flesh, and cold etched its way down his arm.

"Hello, der, Mr. Lincoln. Mr. Frosty wants a word wif you," said a deep, nasal and utterly immovable voice in his ear.

Abe's nerves froze, and the hairs on the back of his neck stood up. Mr. Frosty? Oh shit.

A second, freezing hand grabbed underneath his left armpit, sending sharp, ice-shards crackling through his chest. He tried to scream, but the breath caught in his throat, puffing out from between his lips in a cloud of steam.

"Come along, Mr. Lincoln, you don't want us to 'ave to use the carrot, do you?" said another basal voice.

Abe managed a huff, "Caroline!" he tried, but the journalist was unconscious at his feet. The snowball, which had knocked her cold, was melting by her head.

The two snowmen goons picked Abe up bodily, dragged him out to the ice cream van and drove off.

Mr. Horns bleated, grabbed a washer handle with his mouth, and opened the door. He removed a woolen sock and started to chew.

Amendment 6

The Gyre shall not infringe the right of citizens to converse with pixies. It is advised, however, that pixies are scurrilous, no-nothing, ill-mannered bastards and should not be taken seriously. The Gyre holds it most proper to advance discourse with any other being, as long as they are real. Unreal things should not be talked to, as they don't exist.

The bear snuffled at the bins in the dank alleyway. The sea sloshed in the waterway which separated the two sides of the street. There was no life within the waters, only garbage, oil slicks and rotting vegetation.

The bear's stomach gurgled in hunger, and his nose twitched as he inhaled the rank odors of rotting burger bits and sputum, wafting up from out of the bins. He licked at an unappetizing wrapper, tasting the fish grease and mayonnaise remnants.

The bear's collar chaffed hard against his neck, leaving a sore red ring of cracked and bloody skin. He didn't care, the leather would rot away, eventually. Relief from pain would only be followed by more pain, followed by relief from that pain, and then further pain. What was the point?

The pink bow had disappeared from his head. His owner was no more and would no longer replace it, but the bear felt nothing. His mistress had fed him and had tended to his needs, but had also humiliated him and scrawled satanic tattoos on his flesh.

The feeding and pampering of sorts though; born from affection, depressed him. Both were pointless, simply elongating his minuscule existence. The cruelty to, was only fleeting, a pinprick, outweighed by the fathomless abyss of despair in an uncaring universe doomed to die.

"Fucking hairy bastard!" squawked a pixie, as it straddled a telephone wire.

The bear solemnly gazed up at the pixie with its red-rimmed eyes. The pixie was naked from the waist up, with bright blue skin. It had a large, pointed cap on its head with a little bell on the top which dinged as it leered at the bear and swung its legs idly from its wired perch.

The bear tried to think of a witty comeback, but what was the point? Eventually, everything would be gone, and that included the pixie.

Another pixie hopped down onto the telephone wire and balanced on its tiptoes; walking the wire like a tightrope to get a better look at the bear below.

"Bollocks! Fucking thing ain't that hairy. Look-see, it's all bald in patches." The pixie pointed, and both pixies laughed.

The bear raised himself up onto his hind legs, rearing up to seven feet high.

"Big bugger, init?" scoffed the first pixie.

"Life is a fruitless and pointless journey. Today, I have no fur, tomorrow, no teeth, next week no eyes, and someday no breath. Everything is taken away from us by degrees," signed the bear.

"You're a barrel-full of fucking laughs, I must say," squawked the pixie.

"And you ain't got no fuckin' shoes, neither," laughed the second pixie. The two pixies wiggled and taunted with their own shoes at the bear to make their point.

There was no use arguing with the pixies, he concluded. The cocky little fairy-folk made no sense at the best of times.

"I'm only alive because I lack the motivation to end my own life," he signed.

"A bag of assholes to that!" shouted the first pixie.

"If I suck you off, will you do us a dance?" cackled the second one.

The ill-mannered pixies roared in laughter, swinging back and forth on the telephone wire, and slapping each other on the back.

The bear dropped back to all fours with a huff and wandered off down the alleyway. Sloshing some gutter-water that fell from an open pipe in the shanty building's sides.

The Sun split the sky and shone a warming beam down on his back. He paused for a moment to absorb the warmth. It felt wonderful as the heat soothed the tensions.

"Why do you stress so?" asked The Sun.

"Because the future can hold nothing for us," he signed, raising himself on his hind legs. "It will just be the short struggle to the grave, then inevitable oblivion. Nothing I do matters. Nothing will be there to see or care about it in the long run."

"I will be there," beamed The Sun. "When you finally say goodnight, I will see. I see everything."

The bear felt the warmth of The Sun's breath on his face. It only reminded him of the time when he had not felt that warmth or the time in the future when it would disappear again. He shivered.

"Even you will pass," he signed. "One day, you will grow and grow and grow and consume the Earth. Then, finally, you will explode."

"Are you saying I'm getting fat?" asked The Sun, full of suspicion.

The bear's heart fell. The Sun was just as hollow as everyone else. No one could see the misery around them—the pointlessness. Everyone was happily, blind sheep on their way to the slaughterhouse.

"You are calling me fat, aren't you? Well! I come out just to talk to you, and I must say you've been a barrel of laughs to chat to, and you insult my weight! Screw you, bear!" screamed The Sun.

The sky darkened as The Sun disappeared behind thick clouds.

"Hahahaha! Yeah! Screw you, bear!" sang the pixies from further down the alley.

A door used for a fire escape entrance blasted open ahead of him. A blinding white light spilt across the alleyway in a glowing rectangle. A woman stormed out from behind the door, unsteadily on her feet. Blood trickled down around her ear, leaking out from a gash on her head.

"Where is he?" she asked in earnest.

The bear reared onto its hind legs and signed, "Who?"

"Mr. Lincoln? Someone cold-cocked me with a snowball, cheap bastard goons. I could really use your help."

The bear searched his memory bank for a Mr. Lincoln. Ah, yes, the mayor who had recently been disgraced. Politics didn't interest him much, as it too was ultimately meaningless. Good policies, bad policies all would eventually pass into myth and legend.

"Does it matter where the ex-mayor is?" he asked.

"Of course, it matters, someone kidnapped him," snapped the young woman. "I need him, so I can write my newspaper article; also, he had some dirt on the new mayor being evil, or illegal, or something like that. He said the Gyre was in danger. And all right, Abe Lincoln is a blow-hard windbag who'd sell his own grandmother for an extra vote or a boost in the polls, but he isn't stupid either. He's a purebred politician, and his instincts tell him something is fishy with Mayor Moon. If Abe senses something's a-miss, we'd better pay attention."

"Why me?" signed the bear.

The young journalist looked the bear up and down.

"Well," she began, "you're here for a start. Moreover, whoever took Abe is violent, and you're a seven-foot-tall bear. And, thirdly, if Abe is right and Gyre is in peril, then everyone needs to help. The future is at stake. So, are you coming?"

He sighed. It really didn't matter in the long run. Join a quest to save the Gyre? Sure, why not, it didn't matter. He nodded his great shaggy head.

"Good, now we need a place to start. What can you tell me about this?" The young woman opened her hand to reveal a lump of coal. "This was inside the snowball, which knocked me out."

He sniffed at the piece. His big pink tongue extended, and he licked the coal.

"It smells of carrots, and old clothes," he signed, "but it tastes of syrup, and chocolate, and soft fruits?"

"Ice cream," snarled the journalist.

The bear looked puzzled. The young woman was strange and probably concussed.

"It's a calling button from one of Mr. Frosty's goons. The snowmen kidnapped Abe."

If Mr. Frosty has Abe, thought the bear, then there's no chance of getting him back. It would be pointless even to try.

That was when the world went green.

Amendment 7

The Gyre recognizes that all citizens have a right to vote, and but not necessarily one vote only. The Gyre requires all citizens to exercise their right to vote, whether they wish to or not. Failure to exercise this right to vote will end badly. The Gyre deems citizens to include, people, zombies, animals, dinosaurs and chewing gum. Pixies are excluded from voting as they are scurrilous, no-nothing, ill-mannered bastards and should not be taken seriously (see Amendment 6), also they always scribble obscenities on the ballot paper. Snowmen are not considered people, as they are part of the landscape.

The ice-cold air bit at Abe Lincoln's exposed flesh as the two snowmen dragged him, through the chilled storage warehouse, to face Mr. Frosty.

The distinct, sweet smell of boiling syrup wafted through the air. The vast warehouse still produced ice cream as the legitimate front of Mr. Frosty's empire; but, behind the scenes, the old snowman was selling carbonated carrot juice to kids, illegal low-cost laundry, loan sharking and general syndicated crime.

There wasn't a street corner where Mr. Frosty didn't have a piece of the action. Every two-bit hoodlum or thug eventually could trace his hierarchy back to The Ice-King.

The snowmen dragged Abe, and tossed him, face down, at the icy mob-boss's feet where he sprawled out on the frozen floor. He pushed himself up to his knees, his teeth chattering over the room's freezing temperatures that chilled him to the bones.

"Ah, Mr. Lincoln. How nice it is that you have been able to join us," said the giant snowman.

Mr. Frosty stood well over seven-feet-tall. He wore a dark-blue bowler hat on his massive head. He bore three lumps of coal on his chest as buttons and around his neck was a very expensive red silk scarf. In his mouth, he puffed on an exquisitely carved Meerschaum pipe with a handle made of black ivory: the rich scent of smoke clouded the above his head. His thick sausagey fingers, which were not well defined, were covered in gold signet rings.

A horrid mildew like scent wafted from the snowman's frozen body, which his pipe tobacco's scent failed to mask. He creaked with every movement he made, a sound like a glacier eroding rocks. His eyes were two blank, lumps of coal and his nose was a crooked, half-rotted carrot in which a grimy worm had set up home.

"I have been hearing some disturbing news about you, Mr. Lincoln," continued The Ice-King. His snow henchmen grinned at each other behind him.

There were four henchmen that Abe could see, all tall well-muscled snowmen. Various vegetables were used for noses, and they wore varying amounts of old clothing. They all looked like they could tare Abe apart at a moment's notice if Mr. Frosty said the words.

The mob boss folded his arms behind his back, with a sound like an avalanche, and moved a few steps in Abe's direction. Abe was no longer sure if his shivering was due to the temperature or his fear.

Mr. Frosty was powerful, all snowmen were. The inhuman force of primal snow ran through them. Snow, which would smother a city. Snow, which would rip down powerlines. Snow, which would freeze men to death and laugh at their final heartbeats.

"Mr. Lincoln, I hear you are no longer mayor of our great islands," said Mr. Frosty, in a false tone of camaraderie.

Abe nodded, his teeth chattering. The giant snowman paced back and forth; his massive feet crunched on the hard frosted ground.

"This displeases me," continued Mr. Frosty, icicles forming in his voice. "My organization has invested a lot of money in you and your campaigns. Money, we felt had been wisely spent, money for the future prosperity of everyone. Money, for the new ice cream parlor. Money you took, Mr. Lincoln. And now, we find that all that has been squandered. What do we get for our investment in you, Mr. Lincoln?"

He leaned right into Abe's face.

"We get nothing, Mr. Lincoln. Bupkis. Zip. Nadda. Absolute zero," said the snowman coldly. A cloud of foul, mildew breath blasted Abe in the face.

"Do you know what happened to the last bad investment?" asked Mr. Frosty, calmly smiling. He turned his head slightly to one of his henchmen. "Tell him, Blizzard."

The snowman leered at Abe.

"We gave him the carrot," it growled.

Abe didn't know precisely what "the carrot" was, but his imagination did cartwheels thinking about the possibilities.

"Now, Frosty, come on. This is me, Honest Abe. We... we can still do business," he said, getting to his feet.

"Abe, Abe, Abe," tutted Mr. Frosty, shaking his giant snowball head. "What business? We paid for your election, and now you are of no use to us. You are not in a position to aid our various enterprises. What good are you?"

"My political career isn't finished yet," snarled Abe. "I won't go out this way. Replaced by The Moon?"

The snowman kingpin huffed a laugh. "You don't appear to be getting much choice in it."

"Come on, back me again, Frosty," said Abe, his pulse quickening as he saw the first glimmers in the snowman's coaled eyes.

"You are insane, my friend. Why would I back you?"

Go for broke, thought Abe. *You've got him hooked. He already wants to back you; otherwise, he'd have had you killed and dumped in a marina as a warning to others. He must have tried to reach out to The Moon and got nowhere, and now he's stuck with you. So, Abe, make him believe. Give him a future to aim for.*

It was time to put on the old bullshit routine.

"Back me, because you know I'll owe you big. Because you know I never lose. Because you know in a fair fight, I'd take him. Because you know I won't fight fair. Because you're a gambler, and I'm a good bet. Back me, on the campaign trail, and I'll beat him, and we'll carve up the Gyre, like soft scoop. The ice cream parlor will get built. I promise."

The old snowman smiled. "Abe, you really are a world-class bullshitter. The next regular scheduled election isn't for another two years. Why should I let you live that long?"

He was curious. Abe could see it.

"You won't have to," lied Abe. He had absolutely no idea what he was saying, but his mouth kept running. Give it time, he always knew what he was getting to; by the time he finished his sentences. "They can't just place a new mayor in office. That's not how it works. Sure, they can fire me, but then there should be an election. The council never held an election for the people to vote."

The mob boss leaned back and roared a laugh. "You're going to demand a snap election on them? When?"

"A week," grinned Abe. "The oysters return from their southern migration in a week. That's a portent. I can call for it then."

"A week? You're crazy! You're not prepared," said the snowman.

"Neither are they. That makes it an even playing field. And I am better than them, especially as I'm going to play dirty. I'll call a snap election and hold a great debate against The Moon. Then, we'll all vote. Then, I'll win."

The snowman smiled again. "You've got dirt, haven't you?"

"Enough, and I've got a few tricks left. Give me the money and the time, and I'll bring The Moon crashing down, and we'll be back to the business as usual. Deal?" Abe stuck out his hand.

He could see the future in front of him sharp and crystal clear. He'd get the money. He'd get his election. He'd get to debate The Moon. Sure, it would be hard, but it would be hard politicking, and that's what he did best. He'd show everyone Abe Lincoln was back.

He smiled warmly as he felt Mr. Frosty's icy palm freeze to his.

"Mr. Frosty, you won't regret this."

Amendment Pixie

> *The Pixie King likes it known that the pixie kingdom don't give two shits about humans and stuff. A bag of rotting cow assholes to that. Pixies will take no part in human affairs. You don't want US, we don't want YOU. Pixies are here to renounce all interest with the humans.*

The Pixie King sat on his throne in the palace of Nextworld and cogitated. His backside hurt from the cold stone, and the warts on his face ached. The silver crown he wore on his head grew tight over the centuries, but that was to be expected as he had put on a great deal of weight; well over 10lbs. He was old, very old, and had made his mind up about humans long ago. Now, times were changing, and if you didn't change with them, well, you would probably die.

Around him, his handmaids and guards fucked, or screamed incoherently at the wall, or threw up or did any number of normal fairy-folk activities. The humans would not approve of these behaviors, but humans were weird, anyways.

He wriggled his toes and watched his pet worms slithered nearby. He extended his feet, as far as he could, and felt the warmth from his pet worms, as they sucked the rot from between his toes. His little vestigial wings fluttered with excitement.

"Lord high cock-sure one," said an orange-skinned pixie to The King. "We have transmogrified the ugly one and the big hairy fucker she was with. We brought 'em 'ere, and we didn't fuck 'em up the bum or nothin'. They request to be brought to your most gloriously obese presence."

The Pixie King belched his approval.

"The moment's passion be with you, your highness," said the guard retreating.

The Pixie King waved his regal hand and stuck up two fingers at the guard. The moment's passion be damned; this was about the future.

The prisoners-guests were brought in. The big, ugly girl stood as proudly as a human could do with her arms tied behind her back with knotted sunlight. The big hairy fucker was in chains, although his sunlight collar was around his neck. A pixie guard hovered above holding the leash that attached to the collar, leading the big hairy fucker to the throne room.

"What is the meaning of this?" asked the ugly girl.

"Silence, fuck face!" shouted the guard.

The surrounding guards and handmaids laughed raucously, slapping their thighs, and holding their sides. They grew bored, quickly of laughing and went back to fucking or throwing up. The King didn't blame them—life could be really dull, if you didn't seize the moment.

"Listen, you big lollop," said The King, wiping his greasy hand across where his chin used to be. "We don't have time for nicey-nice, and we don't have time for invites or other things neither. Everything is going to hell in a handbasket."

"No time! No time! No time!" sang the handmaids and guards in parody.

This was good. The handmaids and guards understood the urgency; otherwise, they would not have sung it. They even sang it in harmony and stopped fucking, vomiting or defecating for a few seconds. That was as serious as pixies ever got.

The King readjusted his weight in his chair. Sweat dripped from his forehead, down his back and puddled in his ass crack. He pulled himself up to his full imposing height of one-foot by one-inch.

"Now, listen, Lolloth," said The King.

"My name is not Lolloth," interrupted the ugly girl.

"Shut up!" snapped The King. He slammed his flabby fist down on the arm of his throne. Humans were so weird and protective about stuff to the pixies. "If I says you're Lolloth, then you're Lolloth. Now listen, the grey-skinned, bald fuckers are coming."

The King saw a cloud of bewilderment fall over the ugly human's face. Stupid humans, they never, ever, ever paid any attention.

"Things like that don't exist," said the ugly human, flatly.

"She's a stuuuupid one!" said a handmaid, as a pixie guard entered her doggy style.

"Duh, duh, I's a 'uman! Things don't exist!" cackled a guard as he took to the air and defecated.

The worms at The King's feet sang a lilting refrain, calling up images of the high heather. The King concentrated, biting hard on his flabby lips. There was no time for reverie. Pixies didn't do memories very often and now was a particularly a bad moment.
"Stupid humans," said The King, shaking his fat head. "You never pays attention. They's coming. And when they do it ain't just you lollies which is in the aimin' sights. It's all worlds. It's here too, you big fudge-knuckle."

The girl just looked at The King, her eyes glazed over. A guard in a corner blew a giant raspberry. This was serious as blowing raspberries was a bad sign. The crowd was becoming unsettled.
"I don't understand," said the dumb girl.
The King huffed and tried to speak slowly and carefully. "We needs that friend of yours, that mayor big-wig type, we needs him to be the mayor."
"Abe? Well, he was working on that. He thought The Moon was dangerous for the Gyre, or illegal, or something. But,

44

the Snowmen took him. That's where we were going when you kidnapped us."

The King nodded somberly. "Don't worry about the Snowmen, Lolloth, they won't hurt that mucky-muck. But he knows about how bad that Moony bugger is? Yeah, he ain't quite as dumb-fuckery as the rest of you ugly lots."

"Ugly lots. Ugly lots!" sang the fairy-folk crowd.

"Especially that hairy fucker!" shouted one of the pixies from above.

The big hairy fucker sat back on his haunches, catapulting the pixie guard holding its leash off into the distance. He watched with a glum expression. Then, he raised his hands and started signing.

"He's a big fucker, isn't he?" shouted a handmaid.

"And he's got a great hairy cock!" laughed the guard, as he ploughed the handmaid. "Ah, look-see, the ugly girl's noticed it too. Can't be keepin' her eyes off'n it!"

"You want Mr. Lincoln to be mayor?" signed the bear, ignoring the fairy-folk. "Why? What's the point?"

The King eyed the big hairy fucker. "We need 'im to be the mayor, not that Moony cunt. Old big-wig will do fine as mayor, thank you very muchly."

The big hairy fucker sat for a second. He scratched his ear with a long, sharp claw. "What's the point? It's all immaterial anyway. Lincoln, Moon. Nothing matters. We're all going to die in the end."

"You big, luggerhead!" snapped The King. He reached behind himself, gathered a fistful of ass-sweat and underwear clag and flicked it at the big hairy nitwit. "'Course it matters. Them grey bastards won't be here if that old mayor big-wig is mayor. And they's a problem for everyone – 'umans, fairy-folk, or big hairy dick-bags like you."

The King gave a hacking cough, snorted loudly, and spat the resulting gob on the floor. The worms mewled and sang, snuggling into the lump of mucus.

"Now, let me tell you, Lolloth," said The King, addressing the big ugly girl, "we hopes that old mucky-muck big-wig is getting to be mayor again, with that elector-thingy of yours. That'd solve all the problemos. However, if he don't, well then, we's all bull-fucked."

The ugly human's face creased in confusion as she tried to organize her thoughts.

"So you fairy-folk want Abe to be mayor, and you're hoping that he'll call for an election and win that?"

"You got it, fuck-face!" squealed a handmaid.

"What if he doesn't?" signed the bear. "What if he can't call an election? What if Mr. Lincoln calls it but The Moon wins? It could happen. The only certainty is that this whole thing will end in cold death."

"Fuck cold death," shouted a guard, "let's have hot mead!" It transmogrified to the human world to look for some mead to steal and drink.

"That's what we brought you 'ere for, you great hairy sack of donkey shit!" said The King, addressing the big hairy one. "If he wins that elector-thingy, then bull whizz, drinks all round. But if he fails, or don't get to do that elector-thingy, then we's got problemos."

"Problemos! Problemos!" chorused the fairy-folk court.

The ugly girl and the bear shared a worried look.

"And when we's got a problemo then you ugly 'umans is going to want me and the fairy-folk to be on your side. You's gonna want us to be there. You's gonna want us to fight. That's why I's transmogrified you 'ere – to tell you there is a price."

"A price?" asked the ugly human girl, raising an eyebrow.

"Look Lolloth, we don'ts 'ave to be 'ere. If it do go all to hell in a hand-basket, then the fairy-folk can always close the door."

The girl looked puzzled again.

Stupid humans, they never understood anything or paid attention. The King farted and huffed.

We can shut the gate, close the door, lock all the fairy-folk away in this place, in the Nextworld. Be real quiet-like, and hopes them grey bastards don't comes a-knocking'. But we don'ts want to do that. It well risky. We will, if we has to, but we'd rather not."

"We does what we wants! We does what we wants!" sang the handmaids and guards.

"So, if big-wig chubby-wubby wants the fairy-folk's help, then there is going to be a price," said The King, silencing the crowd with a wave of his toes. "We're gonna wants what the Snowmen wants."

"What do the Snowmen want?" asked the ugly human.

"We want what we wants! We want what we wants!" sang the handmaids and guards in chorus.

"Nah, nah, nah, Lolloth. Naughty, naughty. We'lls discuss it if'n the time comes. Now, fuck offski. Back to the human world with yous."

The King clapped his hands, with a sound like two wet fish slapping together. The guests-prisoners were surrounded by a haze of bright green fire. Then, whompf, they vanished.

"All gone! All gone!" sang the fairy-folk court.

Yes, thought The Pixie King, *all gone. And now, we waits and we sees if old Abe Lincoln can win the mayoral election or whether we're all really fuckeried.*

Amendment 8

The Electorate shall be required to vote upon any issue pertaining to public service positions every span of no more than five years, or the call of an ordinary citizen when the portents deem it fortunate. Portents include: the coming of the blue snow, a pixie making sense, the returning of the oysters, the release of a good U2 album or the second Tuesday in November if the wind comes in from the west.

The recycling plant, Abe had chosen to hold his rally, was vast, metallic, and sweaty. Smelting forges at the end of massive conveyor belts, which took the accumulated waste from the sea, gave off great plumes of heat, coke dust and flame, making the assembled newspaper people and rally supporters slick and grimy. It was noisy place, smoke-filled, and a bit dangerous, and overall, a damn stupid place to hold a rally, but suited Abe's visual purpose.

The old made new, that was what he was going for. A recycled Abe for the recycled Gyre.

The Moon as the new mayor? The Moon was too new. The Gyre was old stuff made fresh, and the Moon didn't fit or belong. That was the angle he was conveying in his campaign. But, in the end, the feeling that the Moon didn't belong did actually worry him.

Abe rated himself as a grade-A, unscrupulous shyster and a purebred son of a bitch who'd rob everyone blind and make them say *"thank you"* for the privilege. However, that was an honest sort of thievery, a straight-up politician's thievery. The kind of theft everyone voted for one way or another every five years.

The Moon was entirely different, strange, and out of place. The journalist had tried to explain her adventures with the Pixie King; something about grey bastards, but she hadn't been able to articulate it. And even now, the memory of her saying it was fuzzy and distant as if it were a dream or just something unimportant which should be forgotten.

A few Pixies sat on the roof beams or swung from suspended cables. Some had cock-shaped ice-lollies which they'd make at home and bring for these occasions.

"Look at all th'm ugly fuckers!" shouted a blue pixie, pointing at the crowd below. "Bet their sweat tastes like marzipan!"

"Give us a kiss, and a rim-job!" cackled a greenish pixie.

Abe scanned the crowd, hoping to see some important people before he started his big rabble-rousing speech. If he was lucky, he'd spot at least one spy from the Council. That'd be good, and that would mean they saw him as a threat.

Instead, he saw Caroline pulling out her ocarina and playing a few notes to describe the scene. She'd given up on writing about it or painting it—this was her new way of composing her article as a musical piece. That kind of annoyed Abe, as he'd spent hours stringing up the wiring system and selecting the phonograph record to entertain and warm up the crowd, and now she wasn't even listening to the music.

The bear sat next to her, who had scared the living-shit out of Abe when he'd found it in her company, grunting and shaking his massive head trying to dislodge some dust and flying insects that he had swallowed.

"You don't like my ocarina either?" Caroline asked.

The bear shook his head but didn't bother to sign. No, he wasn't a music-loving bear, he didn't dance either. The bear didn't do much of anything but follow and drag a permanent cloud with him that blocked out a little patch of sunlight.

Abe continued to scan the crowd. Ordinary human people gathered and larked about, pushing and shoving with their hastily-crafted homemade placards. Abe was pretty sure he hadn't hired all of them, some might be organic "Honest Abe" supporters. Towards the front, there was a gaggle of reporters all with notepads, voice recording snails and high-powered telescopic eagles taking pictures. A small group of zombies shambled in one corner moaning and eating a helpless reporter.

Two tyrannosauruses manned the area. Abe was never quite sure about PC culture pronouns: a van which gave out free roasted cricket legs, covered in barbecue sauce to any who asked. The pair snapped and hissed at each other as they chowed down on their barbecued dripping legs.

A family of crabs were down near the front stage, snapping their pincers in the air, clicking in time with the gramophone music.

Abe noted the fact that none of the Gyre's contingent of headless people, were in attendance. That was a good thing and bad thing. Good, because it meant others were not reminded of his affair. Bad, because the headless voter block of the zombie contingents was significant in the Gyre. To count them as lost votes would be a severe loss to winning any election.

A small group of froggy children giggled and jostled their way to the back of the crowd, heading over an ice-cream truck. The snowmen loitering inside the truck were giving away choc-ices and frozen lollies, they looked muscular and generally threatening.

Ah, yes. The *"deal"* he had made. Well, the Ice-cream parlor was top of the Gyre's agenda already, but he was pretty sure he could hurry it along. There would be many contracts to throw about, and a number of people who he'd owe favors to after all this bullshit was over.

That's all politics was when you got right down to it. Scratch my back, and I'll scratch yours. Selling and buying, who curried favors with who, who had the power to sell, and who wanted to buy.

At the moment Abe was a buyer, but soon enough, he'd be a seller again. He preferred being a seller; a magnanimous father with the power to favor the ones he liked. That suited him. But that was the future—if only he could force it to happen.

Abe changed the wax cylinder on the gramophone, and a wonky skiffle band version of *Keep on the Sunny Side* lolled out over the patiently waiting public.

"Ladies and Gentlemen, boys and girls," A man's voice boomed over the hastily rigged sound system. "Beasts, zombies, dinosaurs, and chewing gum, would you please welcome to the stage Abraham Lincoln!"

Abe strode out onto the stage in his neat black slacks, and a paisley shirt. His collar was undone, and his sleeves were rolled up to his elbows. He looked like a regular guy, maybe about to take his family on a picnic: precisely the image he wanted to portray. Family Abe, forget about Abe in bed with the headless beauty, remember family man Abe, good old Abe, he'd give you the shirt off his back, if you needed it.

Abe waved and beamed and mouthed 'thank you' to the crowd which dutifully cheered, and woof whistled.

One of his paid for people in the crowd ran up to the stage and offered him a barbecue sauce covered cricket leg.

Abe turned his head to one side in a choreographed look of embarrassment and humility. He took the dripping leg and took a big bite from the thigh. To be fair, it tasted pretty good for cheap meat, cooked over gas made to look like a barbecue.

He threw the rest into the recycling fire where it smoked and filled the room with a charred aroma.

"My friends, thank you, from the bottom of my heart. As you well know, a few days ago, I was forced to step down as mayor of this great town."

The crowd mumbled and murmured.

"Yes, friends, I did wrong. I know that, and I apologize. I let you all down."

Come on, he thought, *buy it. Buy my nice, cheap words.*

"Even so, a greater tragedy also befell us all that day. On that day your council of elected officials took it upon themselves to appoint another mayor in my stead. And that was a great injustice, on all of us, it was against the town charter."

The murmuring of the crowd grew.

Follow my lead. Look over there. It's their fault. Not me, them. I'm on your side - I look just like you in my paisley shirt and black slacks. I fed you, pleased you, entertained you. I'm just like you—it's them—they're the elite. I gave. They took.

"The council took your rights away. It should have been your choice, my friends. If you wanted me fired, then so be it. The council should not have removed me and replaced me with The Moon, without consulting you first. That's not fair. That's not in the island's charter. That's not how it's done." Abe raised his fists in the air with each sentiment.

The crowd grew louder.

"But this is the Gyre, and we don't take kindly to the elites making decisions for us. You, the people, are free to decide your own fates. It's you who gets to decide who runs these islands. It's you who gets to decide who's mayor."

The crowd roared.

"He's right!" said a human, Abe had hired to stand in.

"We need to vote!" said another one of his hired standees.

"It's our democratic right!" an unhired organic person yelled.

"My friends, the oysters return at the end of the week. I move that we have an election then. And I also would like to announce my candidacy. I would like to be your mayor, once again."

There was a fury of applause from the crowd chanting, "Abe! Abe! Abe!"

"I have spoken to The Moon, and I find that it is lacking in both human understanding and in its fiscal policy. It will simply not be able to make us great again, not like I can. It is not human. I am one of you and that is why I am running for mayor."

The placards bounced up and down. The crowd clapped and hooted louder.

"I can make the Gyre great again. I will finally complete the eight years in the making: the new ice cream parlor on the corner of Main Street, bringing in jobs and moving us into the 21st century. That is what the Gyre needs, new industry, as well as support for our great recycling plant!"

More whoops and cheers from the crowd.

"Vote for me on Friday for a brighter future. Vote for Abe, and vote for freedom!" Abe finished and dived headfirst into the crowd. The people caught him and carried him aloft like a surfer on the crest of a wave.

There was clapping, whopping, and stamping of feet. There was cawing and flashing from the high-powered eagles as the reporters caught the moment for all posterity, and with a bit of luck it would make the front pages of the evening newspapers.

But Abe realized something was missing. Where was the baby? Every political rally needed to have an accompanying picture of the politician kissing a baby on the cheek. Abe wasn't entirely sure why. Tradition? Empathy? It didn't really matter. It would seal his triumphant return. Luckily, he'd arranged for a "spontaneous" person in the crowd to hand him a baby just for the sake of pictures.

Somewhere off to his right, he saw the small child being carried towards him. With fingers far too long to be human, a spindly grey hand handed the swaddled child up to Abe as he sat on the shoulders of one of the crowd goers.

His mawkish smile symbolized his embarrassment by the attention, but when all the high-powered eagles were facing him, he unwrapped the swaddling baby from the cloth and readied his pose for the pictures.

The baby-thing was a misshapen lump of grey skin, with two pitiless, black, almond-shaped eyes. Its head, if that's what it; was bulbous and the skin on it was sloughing off in large flakes. Abe had held a lot of various species of babies in his political years; from headless ones who gobbed throat phlegm on him, to animal ones who always relieved themselves on him, to zombie ones who monotonously tried to bite him. Yet, he'd never seen anything like this creature.

It writhed and wriggled in Abe's arms, and then a dark pink slash fissured across its face. The rancid pink fleshing inside made no sound, only a stench of rotting seagull intestines.

Abe's animal instincts took over. He screamed and hurled the baby-thing into the recycling center's smelting furnace where the flames quickly consumed it.

As the sweat on his skin started to cool, Abe heard the high-powered eagles' cawing as they took their pictures.

Amendment 9

The Gyre decrees that citizens who have reached adulthood are no longer allowed to throw tantrums. Tantrums are for small children who are unwilling to accept the world's unfairness. Adults may react to problems in the following ways: Drinking whiskey, listening to Rammstein really loud, killing a pixie, sex, glass blowing, yoga, monkey knife fights, yodelling, adoption or war. Please note that only real things can cause problems. Unreal things are unreal and therefore cannot cause problems.

"He did what?!?" gasped the Spokeswoman for Internal Wants.

The Council Member for Budgetary Responsibility eyed the newspaper again. "He threw the baby into the furnace." He peered up over the newspaper. "I don't think that was very responsible."

"I want to know what happened next," replied the Spokeswoman. "Did they arrest him?"

The Council Member for Budgetary Responsibility sniffed and scanned the article again. "Ummmm, errrrr, no. The police did hold him for questioning, but they were unable to charge him with any offence regarding the child, as no one knew who the child was, or who it had belonged to. Abe was given a caution for improper disposal of waste in the recycling furnace and fined ¥50."

"Social Justice!" squeaked the hedgehog as he sucked up a worm from a plate of them in front of him.

The Committee Member for Commitment slammed his fist unto the table. "God damn it. It would have been so much easier if they'd locked him up. Now, we'll have to commit to there being an election."

The Moon, who sat at the head of the council table, rolled gently in the chair. Its face turned a darker, more sallow cream-color, and made an odd grinding noise. Everyone agreed mentally and recognize this as displeasure.

"Social Justice?" squeaked the hedgehog with an apologetical tone.

"Of course, we all want there to be no election, Mayor Moon," said the Spokeswoman for Internal Wants. "But it's likely to be out of our hands. It is in the island's charter that he can call one when the oysters return, and they are due at the end of the week."

The Moon grew a darker, browner color, and its grinding noise got louder. It rotated so that its Mare Frigoris was facing the assembled members.

"Don't show your cold side Mayor Moon," said the Council Member for Budgetary Responsibility. "Abraham Lincoln is coming, and he has regrettably, called an election. His poll numbers are low, and this baby furnace incident will not have helped that, so we must capitalize on it. What we need now is a plan and a responsible budget to fund your campaign."

"Social Justice!" squeaked the hedgehog in excitement.

"I propose that we delay the building of the new ice cream parlor for another quarter," continued the Council Member for Budgetary Responsibility.

There was a general nodding no one spoke up in favor, but no one opposed it either. That had been the case for each quarter for the last eight years, the money always being siphoned toward something else.

"With the budgetary surplus created by postponing the parlor's building, we will be able to fully fund your campaign."

The Moon beamed happily and rolled for the next motion.

The Committee Member for Commitment stood up. "My gentle colleagues," he smiled, with easy charm. "I would like to raise a point of order. As Committee Member for

Commitment, it is my responsibility to make sure that we are committed in all senses of the word."

He ran his hands through his thick, lustrous hair, making the Spokeswoman for Internal Wants want something internal very rapidly.

"To that end, I have taken it upon myself to find a wife for our friend, The Council Member for Budgetary Responsibility. I have spoken with him privately, and he is totally committed to this as well."

The Spokeswoman for Internal Wants applauded loudly. This was a good move. Her eyes roved to the Council Member for Budgetary Responsibility's finger. She could see the old patch of worn skin where a ring had until recently resided. Nevertheless, since there was no ring, then the Council Member could not have ever been married, that stood to reason.

There was something else, and she wanted to remember what it was. Something about the Council Member having a wife only the other day, but that was silly. People didn't just disappear. And other people certainly didn't forget or ignore people who disappeared.

"Social Justice!" squeaked the hedgehog.

The Spokeswoman for Internal Wants felt a cold stare on her shoulder. The Moon had turned in its seat and was looking straight at her, its vast, glowing face illuminating her. She saw its craggy features in all their glory, The Ocean of Storms, The Sea of Fertility, the Tycho crater. The Moon seemed to stare into her very soul, nosing into her thoughts and wishes.

The Moon's questing mind probed and poked inside her head, riffling through her memories like a librarian checking for a lost book. Her childhood memories were trashed, tranquil thoughts of her father smashed, sexual encounters were ravaged then discarded. The Moon's sticky fingers were in her mind. She smelled hot dogs, runny bathwater, and toast, and forensic science laboratory equipment.

The fingers found what they were looking for, a squishy train-worm of thought and logic. The Spokeswoman for Internal Wants felt those thoughts crushed in her mind. The Moon's fingering-thought power pulled back from her brain. She felt the hole inside her mind, that had been left behind, like a missing tooth in a gum line.

Lights shimmered in one corner of the council chamber, and two spindly figures materialized from the damp, crab-shit heavy air. Grey and sexless, with large almond eyes and bulbous heads, they loitered in the corner.

Darkness fell across The Moon's face as it started to eclipse. Shadowy fissures revealed themselves within the craggy lunar surface as it turned and exposed the spires and technology on its unlit side.

The spindle figures advance towards the group. One reached behind its back and produced a metal cylinder. The Committee Member for Commitment stood stock still, open-mouthed as the spindly figure pointed the ray gun at his chest and pulled the trigger.

The Committee Member was hauled into the air, as if on a wire. His mouth opened in a silent scream, veins bulging out all over his body. The lustrous, weeping scars on his forehead erupted, spilling a stinking, oozing a creamy pus. His eyes flipped to a milky white and a foul smell of burning hair and crisping pig flesh filled the council chamber. His skin blackened and flaked away until there was nothing, but a pile of dust.

The other councilors sat, stunned. The Committee Member for Commitment was just a pile of ash and teeth. The spindly figures strode forward. One extended a long-gnarled hand and pulled a few teeth from the ex-Committee Member for Commitment's dust pile. A blood-red tear, split across its face, revealing a chasm of pink awfulness within, accompanied by a rotting stench of seagull intestines.

A small squeak escaped the Spokeswoman for Internal Wants as the spindly figure jammed the teeth into its newly formed maw. It bit down hard, then clicked its new teeth into place and smiled.

"Social Justice?" asked the hedgehog in a soft voice.

The smiling figure sat in the empty council seat and clicked its new teeth twice. It reached over to the Social Justice Hedgehog, who quivered in fear. Gently, it pulled out a single spine from the mammal's back. The hedgehog squeaked in surprise.

Slowly, the grey figure scratched a sign onto its forehead. Thin, inky-black blood ran down from the wound, covering its grey skin. It finished and revealed a question mark.

The Spokeswoman for Internal Wants and the rest of the council members ignored the interloper. Aliens did not exist therefore, it couldn't be there, and the Committee Member for Commitment couldn't have just disintegrated. And, since he clearly couldn't have been disintegrated, but also was now a pile of dust, then he couldn't have existed QED.

The Moon lit up again, as its eclipse passed. Its craggy features once again, graced the councilors.

The door opened at one end of the room and a velociraptor entered. Its reptilian head bobbed one way, then another as it scanned the councilors. It screamed and clicked its sharp toe-claw on the floor, then approached the table and hastily passed a note to the Council Member for Budgetary Responsibility. Its stare snapped up from the note and it scanned the members at the table again. Its gaze hung on the stranger who sat in the empty chair, the stranger who couldn't possibly be there. The stranger clicked its teeth twice. The velociraptor blinked, chirruped like a bird, then retreated through the door into the dark alcove.

The Council Member opened the note and read. A frown crossed his sullen, sunken, bachelor-face. The Spokeswoman for Internal Wants felt a pang of pity for him, it was a shame he had never found a wife or had anyone to help him find one.

"Fellow...errr...members," he said, hastily glancing to the seat occupied by the alien, "I have some grave news. Abraham Lincoln has issued a challenge of a grand debate, whereby our illustrious Mayor Moon and himself will go head-to-head, debating their various visions of the future of the Gyre."

The strange councilor clicked its teeth. Everyone ignored it.

The Moon looked uncertain for a moment. The strange councilor, who could not really be there, clicked his teeth again. Everyone ignored it.

The Moon looked at his councilors steadily, then nodded in acquiescence. And so, it would be: a great debate and then a vote to decide the fate of the Gyre.

Abe versus The Moon.

Amendment 10

Opinion polls may not be undertaken between the electorate and the people running for government office. The electorate may lie, ignore the question, write rude replies, or deface in some way the paper on which the poll question is stated, and therefore it is unreliable. Also, it smacks of hubris to ask the public their opinion and then ask them to repeat it by voting.

The advert blinked and flitted on the old, faded cream-colored television as it hung in one corner of Dyno's Diner like a giant spider sitting on its web. Copper wires and cabling dangled out the back; the poor attempt of an aerial was held together with bits of twine. The image it tried to convey in fuzzy black and white static, kept flicking on the screen as the tuning was ever-so-slightly wonky.

Dyno, who owned the diner, was a brontosaurus. He was definitely a Brontosaurus, a thunder lizard and not an Apatosaurus nor a Diplodocus, who had nothing to do with thunder. There was nothing wrong with being either an Apatosaurus or a Diplodocus, some of his best friends were Diplodoci, but he was resolutely a Brontosaur, and he made sure everyone knew that was what he was—tradition and knowing where you came from was crucial.

The diner was not very busy, even for a Tuesday night. Business had been slow for a while now, and Dyno was not sure how he was going to keep going unless things picked up soon. He'd agonized over letting two of his waiting staff go, but he'd done it, making the entire team just him and one Dilophosaur chef, who cooked the spiced dishes using her own poison. The diner currently had only one patron in it, but Dyno was confused about that too.

His eyesight was weak, and he stared blearily at his one and only customer. It certainly had feathers, so it might have been one of the council velociraptors, but when it had entered, Dyno could have sworn it walked far too upright to have been a dinosaur. In fact, he was sure it had walked like a man, but that would have been silly, no humans ever came into a dinosaur establishment, it simply wasn't a thing that happened.

The probable-velociraptor sat in a booth in a corner and skooched down to try and make it seem like it wasn't there. It was all very untraditional behavior, Dyno thought as he slowly stretched his long neck over and chinned the television to try and improve the reception.

"Mr. Brains', Brainz! For the zombie on the go!" the advertisement from the television chimed.

The screen went blank, and then a voiceover said, "There now follows a campaign commercial by Mayor Moon."

From his booth, Abe Lincoln hissed at the mention of The Moon and tried to readjust his disguise. He peeked out from between the jaws of his headdress to peer up at the Moon's broadcast.

The advert started with pictures of people, all holding placards with slogans along the lines of "*Mayor Moon get it done*" and *"Abe Lincoln? NO WAY!"*

A voiceover broke in, a harsh raspy voice, dry, as if he swallowed a clump of dust from a tomb. "Mayor Moon is building a movement to replace the failed governance of the corrupt Lincoln establishment."

The images changed to long lines of unemployed people, almost all human, with some scattered dinosaurs and zombies thrown in for good measure.

"The failed government of old Abe has left the Gyre high and dry. Jobs are disappearing, people are getting poorer, this great Gyre of ours is dying, bled dry by an elite that simply doesn't care for ordinary hard-working folks."

Faux placards with Pro-Abe wording were thrown on the ground, and people trampled across them.

"And the only way to stop this corruption, this decay, this naked war against the Gyre, is you, is us, is our movement, is The Moon."

The screen showed a full shot of the Moon in all its lunar glory.

"When the oysters come, give old Abe the finger."

There were several images of people giving the bird directly to the camera.

Dyno honked in laughter at that.

"And give Mayor Moon your vote," finished the advert.

The screen flashed, "ABE LINCOLN BURNED A BABY— *VOTE MAYOR MOON*", a stark white lettering on a black background for a full ten seconds. Then the advert cleared.

Abe snarled to himself. It wasn't the best advert in the world, but it was effective. Give your vote to the Moon and the finger to Abe, damn, he should have thought of that.

Where was his contact? They should have been here over an hour ago, he thought.

Grumbling in frustration, Abe took a sip of his Jungle Juice, it tasted like it was meant to be—swamp water. Why had he suggested meeting in a Dino diner? He knew they only served dinosaur food and drink, which was unpalatable to any human. But then, it was the last place people would be expecting to find him.

"Mr. Lincoln?" came a hushed voice from somewhere below the table.

Abe paused for a moment. "...Yes, is that you Mint-Throat?" he asked, uncertainly.

"Did you bring the money?" There was a faint aroma of spearmint wafting up from under the table.

Abe pulled out the brown envelope from his sleeve. It was stuffed full of bills, representing most of the "investment" from Mr. Frosty.

"Place it under the table," said the spearmint voice.

Abe did as instructed and felt a manilla folder drop onto his knee.

"Inside, Mr. Lincoln," said the hushed voice, "you will find all the polling data from The Moon's camp, and some fresh polling conducted by my associates. It has been a pleasure doing business with you once again. You know how to contact me if you need anything further."

Cautiously, Abe slit the folder open with a letter knife he had in his pocket, pulled out the sheets from the folder and checked the polling data on them. It looked genuine enough. There were some surprising results. Equality was high on the animal voter's minds? Hmmm, that was interesting, Abe pondered. And job creation was still an underlying issue for everyone. Well, that wasn't really rocket science. There were also strong feelings of disunification and disconnectedness for dinosaurs, zombies and humans. Perhaps Abe could pitch himself as the Gyre candidate against the ethereal Moon, that was worth considering.

He hadn't heard a sound from beneath the table for quite some time. Abe decided to sneak a peek.

He found no sign of the money envelope or trace of Mint-Throat, either on his shoe or stuck to the underside of the table. Now, that was a professional.

Amendment 11

The Gyre deems it proper that all elections be held freely and fairly, and all advertising should also be free and fair. Debates between leading candidates, for all government offices, may be held before an election can go ahead. Debates can only be held between real people; unreal things may not debate. A single debate may last no more than four years, as everyone will have died. Death should not be encouraged as an ending of debates. A designated Master of Ceremonies shall be appointed for all debates. The Master of Ceremonies must be a real person. Unreal things may not be Master of Ceremonies as they don't exist.

Bernadette Adams was dead and had been deceased for quite some time. She straightened her pencil skirt and tried to ignore the worms, which slithered and gnawed at her decomposing intestines. She stuck a Biro in her mouth, chewed the end off and drank down the ink.

The ink calmed her nerves. She hoped that the worms would not burst through her flesh at an inopportune moment, that would be hideously embarrassing. Almost as bad as if she let the brain-lust take over, and she went on a killing spree.

Brains! The words grizzled around inside her. She stomped the thought down. She did not need to eat brains. That was what bad zombies did.

The stage was large and had a huge curtain with an emblem of an eagle attacking a crab emblazoned on it. The two opposing lecterns were to either side of a sizeable chocolate fountain version of Botticelli's Birth of Venus. There were several real crabs, scuttling and frolicking over the chocolate fountain. They clutched flags in their claws, a few showing pictures of The Moon, most showing Abraham Lincoln's face poorly drawn in crab scribbles.

Bernadette ignored them. The stupid crabs did have a vote, but they always made up their minds early. She turned as the mayor's representatives bustled in.

"Yes, I understand. It is something that we all want, especially The Moon. He was only expressing that want to me the other day!" clucked The Spokeswoman for Internal Wants into a mobile phone.

"Social Justice!" squeaked her companion.

"Right, got to go, I want to have the meeting about the debate set up now, goodbye!" The Spokeswoman for Internal Wants clicked the phone shut, threw it to the floor and stamped on it.

"Spokeswoman. Hedgehog," said Bernadette, in a graveyard growl.

"Ms. Adams," smiled The Spokeswoman.

"Social Justice!" squeaked the hedgehog.

The nearby crabs scuttled happily. A pair broke away from the others. One of the crabs reaching inside its shell to retrieve a cowboy hat. The other pulled out a Native American feathered head crest, and they started having a gunfight with toy pistols.

Another wave of nausea hit Bernadette. The worms were very restless today.

Brains!

And her inner zombie was very insistent too.

"We wait for Mr. Lincoln's representatives. Then we start the negotiations for debate," growled Bernadette.

"No need to wait," boomed a voice. "I'm here."

Abe strutted across the stage accompanied by a black bear and another young woman, clutching an ocarina.

Bernadette's dead eyes were drawn to the pulse of blood in the woman's throat. She felt her hunger rise—the need to feed on...

BRAINS!

She squashed the thoughts and poured a pen-full of ink down her throat.

She growled, then asked, "Are these two representatives?"

Abe's face clouded with anger. "I do not need representatives. Who better to represent me than me?"

The bear sat on his haunches and began to sign with his forepaws. "In the end, it is immaterial if anyone represents anyone. All will die. Abe, you, and I all come to dust. If Mr Lincoln wishes to represent himself why not indulge him, it does no harm…it does no good either."

"Very well, represent yourself," she said. It was not unheard of, but it was unusual, and a bit pig-headed. "The debate goes as follows, short opening speeches from both candidates, then the audience will ask questions. Neither candidate will know questions beforehand, no psychics either of you. When oysters arrive, the debate is over, and voting begins."

She gave them both a dead-eyed stare.

"We want this too," nodded the Spokeswoman for Internal Wants.

"I assume the questions will be random?" asked Abe.

"The most random we can supply," said Bernadette.

"Every question is pointless," signed the bear. "Why bother to know anything? All questions add up to the cold, hard, reality of an empty and desolate universe with no god or afterlife."

The girl with the ocarina slapped the bear on its side. She reached around and muzzled the bear, inserting a piece toffee inside his mouth. A serene expression flitted across the bear's face and then returned to his normal sullen glower.

"Now, positioning," continued Bernadette. She raised a gnarled, dead finger and pointed at the two podiums. Her bones cracked and snapped, like dried twigs. "What are your wishes?"

"Social Justice!" squeaked the hedgehog.

The whole group turned and stared at the excited mammal.

"We can't accommodate that," she said, "it's too hard, and we have to change too much."

The hedgehog looked crestfallen but didn't repeat the request.

The Spokeswoman for Internal Wants straightened her blouse. "We want the right hand one."

Abe cut her off. "No deal," he growled. He turned and pointed at the back curtain. "The right is the side with the eagle. I won't be the crab in this debate."

The crabs in the fountain stopped and stared up at him.

"Sorry, guys," he apologized.

The crabs, who had been holding the Lincoln flags, dropped them in disgust. Bernadette felt the worms ooze and squiggle in solidarity within her dead innards.

The Spokeswoman for Internal Wants shook her head, "Abe, Abe, be reasonable."

Bernadette stepped in, it was her job as master of ceremonies, after all.

"The incumbent mayor stands at the podium on the right. It is tradition." She ignored his look of disgust as a maggot crawled from around her eyeball and dropped onto her cheek.

"Indeed, that's my point," he said, putting his hands on his hips. "I am the incumbent mayor."

The Spokeswoman for Internal Wants huffed. "You were fired."

"Social Justice!" squeaked the hedgehog.

"Social justice, indeed!" mocked Abe. "The Moon was never properly instated; that's the whole nub of the argument. I am still the incumbent mayor until a duly elected replacement is found." He scoffed and crossed his arms across his chest.

"The Moon wants the right podium," said the Spokeswoman for Internal Wants.

The crabs clicked their claws and pulled out flags of Moon.

Abe stumped his foot. "No deal, I'm not the crab in this debate." He looked apologetically at the crabs in the fountain. "I'm sorry not to choose you fellas, but you're up against an eagle here."

A few crabs shrugged and put away their Moon flags; crabs always knew what they were. Yet, there were still no crabs waving Lincoln flags.

"Oh, come on, guys. I need to be seen under the eagle," whined Abe.

The crabs stared at him and clicked their pincers. A few of them picked up and waved their Lincoln flags.

Abe threw back his head and sighed. "Fine, I'll have the crab side."

The Spokeswoman for Internal Wants beamed as her want was fulfilled.

"Social Justice!" squeaked the hedgehog.

"I hate you guys," huffed Abe at the crabs. Every single crab waved Lincoln flags at him and clicked their pincers happily.

Bernadette ignored them. The crab vote always ended up partisan, and they typically made up their minds for stupid reasons.

"Now, opening theme songs, both have expressed a wish to have them played by The Rolling Stones. This is against the rules. One band, one opening song."

"We will not budge on this want," declared the Spokeswoman for Internal Wants.

There was a kerfuffle from the fountain. The crabs pulled out a very small three-piece drum set, double bass and kazoo. They bobbed their eyes at Abe, knowingly.

"Oh, for fuck's sake!" shouted the ex-mayor.

Amendment 12

The Gyre shall make no law, or laws pertaining to the free exercise therefor of magic to solve problems. The Gyre highly recommends that magic not be used to solve problems as it always causes more issues than it solves, and it invariably means obtaining the services of a pixie. Pixies are scurrilous, no-nothing, ill-mannered bastards and should not be employed in such a fashion (see Amendment 6). If you do, be it on your own head, you have been warned.

He was the crab. He was the goddamn crab. Abe stared hopelessly at the poster of the upcoming debate, rage fomenting inside him, pacing up and down the dressing room he'd been assigned.

There, emblazoned for all to see, in vivid technicolour, was his face under the crab symbol: the symbol that depicted "the loser."

Defeat is how Abe saw it. He felt the foundations of his campaign crumbling away beneath him. That sickly, tingling feeling crackled between his pores, electrifying his toes, adrenaline buzzing around inside his brain.

This was not going well; he could already tell. He'd lost the right to be the eagle. He'd have to make up for that, somehow. What were the statistics? Something like 75% of the time, the eagle side won the vote. Those were terrible odds.

He needed something the voters wanted, or he'd be dead meat in the debate. He had the illegal polling data, which told him the points to promise. But still, he needed a cutting edge, he needed authenticity.

Abe stared at his reflection in the mirror, his eyes looked copasetic, reasonably bright. He'd managed to get half an hour's sleep after the meeting with the master of ceremonies before his nerves had kicked in.

Abe hawked back a great glob of phlegm, spat into a tin of black shoe polish and dragged a comb full through his hair. He hated having to do this, but his hair would soon be turning the white from old age. One's hair could never be too black, sleek, and shiny when stepping up to a podium, ready to debate.

"Has ye done makin' yourself look pretty, you great big-bollocked twat?"

A tremendously fat pixie had appeared in the mirror's reflection right beside Abe's hand. Startled from the pixie's sudden appearance, Abe dropped the tin of shoe polish. He was even more worried to discover that the pixie was only by his hand in the reflection, but when he looked down at his hand the pixie was not an actual reality.

"Figured it out yet, you lanky cum-drip?" asked the fat pixie.

"You're the Pixie King?" said Abe.

"Well, look at that! Ain't you just the smartiest lollygagger!"

"And..." continued Abe, a bit more hesitantly, "you're in the mirror's reflection but not here." He waved his hand where the Pixie King wasn't, just for emphasis.

"See, I thought you was a clever bunny. Well done, big chubby-wub. I ain't with you, I's in the Nextworld still, savvy?"

Abe didn't know, but he nodded anyway.

"So, what can I do for you?" he asked. When the day had started, he had not thought he'd ever be asking that of a pixie, but here he was, Abe the enabler.

"Askes not what yous can does for us, but rather what us can does for you," said the King Pixie tapping his fat nose with a flabby finger.

"Pardon?"

"You's lost your mojo, ain't you – you're dick swing's all gone wrong. That Moony cunt chucked a baby at you, and granted you threw that baby in the fire, and now you's gone all soul searchy."

Abe took a few seconds to try and decipher the strange pixie dialect. Pixies really were mad buggers.

"Well, I am concerned that the campaign isn't going well. There was the baby incident, and the Moon's advert strategy seems to be cutting through, and now I'm placed as the crab in the critical debate."

He pointed at the debate poster over his shoulder; with his face pictured directly under the crab.

"See? You know how often the crab loses? All the time, that's how often! So, yeah, I'm nervous. And a nervous debater is a debater who is going to lose. And that makes me more nervous. I need to be like the Abe on the poster. The go getter, the guy who gives the voters what they want. I need to be the guy everyone loves."

The Pixie King looked at him quizzically. "And yous thinking that be what the islands is needing? Yous being a total shit will make the ugly 'umans and all the o'ffer nut-balls vote you to be big-chief-wiggly-bum?"

"Yes," said Abe, ignoring half of what the pixie was saying: pixies were scurrilous know-nothing bastards, "performing on stage in front of everyone and winning the debate will undoubtedly make people vote for me to be the mayor."

"Yous really thinking that what's them dumb voting buggers needs now, is more lies and bullshittery?"

Abe paused for a moment. Did the various peoples of the Gyre need that?

"Yous know what, fuck it! We's said we'd help and yep we's gonna do just that. You wanting the Billy-big-bollocks Abe Lincoln? Well, you's got him."

The Pixie King snapped his fingers, and Abe felt something grasp his thumb. The pixie faded from the mirror's reflection, as the Abe on the poster tugged Abe's thumb, using it as a lever to pull itself out of the poster.

The pictured Abe snapped out of the poster, unfolding and stretching until he stood eye to eye with Abe. His face lit up with recognition, and an easy-going smile broke from ear to ear.

"Hello there, voter."

"What's going on?" Abe spluttered.

"I'm here to do the debate. I'm here to beat the Moon and win back the mayorship of the Gyre. I'm here to save the day," winked the Poster-Abe.

Poster-Abe snaked its arm around Abe's shoulder and pulled in him close.

"I can see it all now. We're gonna ride this town, friend, ride it hard and fast. We'll win the election, and then it'll be back to the good old times. The power, the money... the girls." The other Abe smiled like an alligator. "We'll do whatever it takes. We'll promise them everything, take what we want, and stiff 'em on the bill. It's gonna be glorious!"

Abe felt clammy, and sticky in the other Abe's presence. He was invading his personal space, all buddy-buddy, a sickly-sweet scent belted Abe across the face, the scent of fake and inauthentic.

"Are you sure...?" he started. Was this, what people wanted? Was this what he wanted? Was this who he actually was, an oily seller of false hopes and bullshit?

Well, maybe. But surely, he was better than this. This seemed so obvious, so fake, so gaudy, like a gold-plated toilet.

"Yeah," said the other Abe, slapping him on the back. "Of course, all we need is a little start-up. Lend me ¥50 to grease the wheels, and we'll be motoring by the end of the evening."

"I've already bribed everyone who can be bribed," Abe blurted.

"Oh, come on, man, just ¥50. Fine, make it ¥20, and I'll make do. I'll give you the shirt off my back if that'll help."

Hey, that was his line, but then again, this was him... *wasn't it?*

He pushed his doppelganger away. "No, I'm not giving you money," he said.

This wasn't right, this wasn't right at all. The man's hair was too greasy and black as if it'd just been rendered in ink. His smile was too clean, his lips just swept across his teeth without flawless. His suit was pressed and neat, but far too neat. Everything was perfect, and that made him look wrong.

"Who are you?"

The doppelganger smiled too innocently. "I'm you, only a bit more confident. I'm the you who can win."

"You're not me," said Abe, lying to himself. "I'm not this slimy thing. I'm better than that. I have integrity!"

The doppelganger burst out laughing. "That's so adorable that you think that. Oh, Abe, I am you—100% the real you, just the more confident bit."

The doppelganger's grin turned to a frown, as he saw Abe's speculating facial expression of disbelief.

"Fine. Stay here. I'll go out, do some canvassing and then I'll win this debate for you. You really wouldn't get anywhere without me, would you?"

Abe was taken aback, as his doppelganger stormed off. What was happening? Only a second ago he was after money and now he was off to go canvassing…?

Abe quickly caught up to his doppelganger and watched him from afar, earnestly talking to a human-stage flunkies. "Come on now, for honest Abe," said the doppelganger, his arms pinning the guy almost to the wall.

"Mr. Lincoln, I don't think I should lend you any money," said the stage flunky, hesitantly.

Is that who I am, thought Abe, *someone who shakes down others for money? Is that really all I am?*

"Well," sighed the doppelganger, "then I'll just take something else."

He pulled a letter knife from his inside suit pocket and plunged it into the stage flunkies' thigh. The doppelganger pulled the blade out and dropped to his knee, lapping at the blood gushing from the flunkies' thigh. The stage-flunky tried to move, and push the doppelganger's face from his suckling grasp, but it was too strong. The doppelganger reached up and pinned the flunkies' arms to the wall as he continued to suck at the gaping wound.

Amendment 13

The right of a person to be a singular entity shall not be violated. No person should be copied, duplicated, or replicated without their knowledge and consent. No court may order such a copying, duplication or replication of any person be it by writ, order, injunction. Honestly, copying of people is at best confusing, and at worst highly likely to be evil, and it happens more than it should—so knock it off, citizens.

"What the hell did you do?" quacked Abe as his doppelganger removed his mouth from the wound.

He smiled a bloody smile, gore dripping from his lips. "Relax, Abe. I bet we won't even lose a single vote."

"What did you do to my leg?" groaned the man.

"I haven't done anything to your leg," said the doppelganger wiping blood from his lips. "It was like that when I got here."

Abe staggered into the mess of blood, already pooling at the man's feet.

"You... you're gonna kill him?"

A disappointed look crossed the doppelganger's face. "Nonsense, I only took what I needed. He's only a voter, and probably a Moon voter anyway."

The man slumped down to the ground; his face turned a ghostly pale colour.

The other Abe stood up, discarding the bleeding man to his fate. The man began to fall into an unconsciousness struggle, blinking a few times before his eyes closed.

"He's going to bleed out!" snapped Abe. "Help me make a tourniquet out of something!"

Blood welled up around his fingers as he tried to apply pressure to the wound. The other Abe wasn't helping; instead, he was walking away. There was something in the doppelganger's hand—it was a wallet and not Abe's own wallet.

Abe's panicking mind put two and two together: the bastard had stolen the guy's wallet too.

Casually, the other Abe walked away down the corridor as Abe tried to staunch the stabbed victim.

SPRANG!

"Well, this is a fine bunch of cock-daisies, init?" The Pixie King was by Abe's knee, leaning on a twisted hawthorn walking stick, his tiny vestigial wings flapping uselessly on his broad back. "Looksee like that big, chubby-wubby you ain't what these islands need, eh?"

"He just stabbed the guy, and stole his wallet," said Abe still in shock.

"Nope," said the Pixie King, poking Abe's knee with his stick. "You didid that. He's you, you big fuck-knuckle. He's only doing what yous do all the timeings—taking people, bleeding them and tossing them aside."

"I... I don't do that!" Abe stumbled his words, which was unconvincing even to himself. Of course, he did that; that was precisely what he did, he used people, he drained them of money or influence, and when he was done with them, they were thrown aside. The gnawing realisation of being exposed ate at his innards. This was him, this other Abe knew him, knew all his secrets, and revelled in them.

Money, girls, power: the other Abe would consume all of them, just as he did, only far, far worse. He pictured it in the other Abe's eye only moments ago, a raging, unquenchable fire of hedonism. Abe saw himself, and he didn't like the picture.

"Un'erstand now, piss-dick?" said the Pixie King, seeing the soul-searching look play out across Abe's face. "These islands don't be needing that Abe Lincoln, any more than they need that Moony cunt. Yous gotta be better than that, un'erstand crab breath?"

"What am I going to do about this guy?" asked Abe as he continued to press down on the stage-flunkies' leg wound. It surprised him that he actually did care about someone else, but it was true, he really didn't want the stage flunky to die, it was kind of his mistake that had caused all of this.

"Yon spinny fuck?" said the Pixie King gesturing at the guy. "Don't flap your little brain about it. I's got the magics, init? I'll take care of him."

The King wiggled his fingers over Abe's bloody hand. Abe felt an odd sensation, as the wound began suckling inwards, like a fish out of water. He pulled his hands away and saw the slashed leg wound binding together as the Pixie King's magic healed the wound.

"Now, stop bein' the twat-burger you is, and start bein' the twat-burger I thinks you can be. Go after Billy-big-bollocks and bring him down before he spreads his shit everywhere and we's all fuckeried."

Abe was a little reluctant to leave the stage-flunky with the Pixie King, but he guessed the magic worked, since blood was no longer oozing out the flunkies' leg.

He stumbled to stand and raced down the corridor following the other Abe's trail. It wasn't as if he could sense his other self, but he knew where he would go next; because he was him—even if he was the him, he no longer wanted to be.

As he galloped down the corridor, he passed groups of bewildered-looking people, animals, and dinosaurs.

"Hey, where's my wallet?" he heard as he passed.

"That was totally inappropriate to touch me there, Mr. Lincoln," said a woman as he sped by.

"Which way did I go?" he asked a particularly startled Styracosaurus. A "gurumph" huffed from his mouth and it indicated a direction with its nose horn.

Abe dashed down the corridor and saw himself in the atrium leaning in close over a headless girl. His doppelganger appeared to be 'trying his luck', but from this distance, it didn't look like the girl was interested, in fact, she looked decidedly uncomfortable.

Oh, God, was that what he looked like when he talked to girls? Like some decrepit stalk seeking a morsel of food in a pond?

He was all bones and elbows, there was no grace, no line, no poise, which were things he'd always assumed he'd had. His skin was so leathery and wrinkled, and his veins stood out blue all over his hands. Beads of sweat dripped down the sides of his face. His Adam's apple jutted from his throat and bobbed up and down as he talked; he couldn't take his eyes off it.

Abe watched his doppelganger heave over the headless girl, reaching his hand casually under her skirt. He hiked up the skirt, exposing the girl's thigh. The girl's legs crossed, instinctively, at the doppelganger's impurity, poisonous-loving stroke.

He saw himself somehow, reflected in this other Abe's vision. He was a lewd, lecherous thief: a user, a pusher, a swindler, and a murderer.

He paused at that last accusation, but the Pixie King was right. Either by action or inaction, during his ruthless climb and his mayoral life, he was ultimately culpable in countless deaths. Worst of all, he'd never even thought about it. This callousness event was suddenly chomping at him.

He was a monster.

"No more!" he snorted to himself. This was not how he was going to be remembered, this was not how history would see him.

He straightened himself up, made a mental note to remember to cite it as 'girding up his loins' for the no doubt bestselling biography, and proceeded toward his doppelganger.

"Let her go, Abe."

Doppelganger Abe snarled, as the headless girl ducked out from under its arm and disappeared around a corner.

"You were supposed to stay in the dressing room," hissed the doppelganger.

"That's the thing about us, Abe, we're good at giving orders but very bad at following them."

Angrily the doppelganger glitched and shot up onto Abe, grasping its hands around his neck, trying to choke him out. Spit flew from Abe's lips as its fingers dug into Abe's neck. Abe's short breaths turned into an agony, as his air began to throttle out of him. His lungs burned, and he saw pulsing red lines at the end of his vision's reach.

Luckily, Abe had never been a fighter in the physical sense, and neither was this Abe. With slow determination, he pried the doppelganger's fingers from around his throat, leaving behind deep red welts where its nails had dug in. He shoved with one knee and was surprised to feel it connect with something fleshy. The other Abe stumbled backwards and fell to the ground grabbing at his crotch.

Abe panted, trying to draw in cool breaths of air into his abused lungs.

"You kicked me in the balls! You dick!" said the other Abe. "That's not cool!"

Abe moved forward to comfort his other self, and that was when the sucker punch came. The doppelganger's fist connected along his eyebrow and the world around Abe went to a thundering scarlet shade. He snapped out of the daze and found himself sprawled on the floor, the other Abe sitting on his chest, drawing back his fist for another walloping

He managed to block the ungainly downward punch by throwing his arm straight up. The other Abe's hand connected with the floor, and he let out a howl of pain and rage.

"Why won't you just go away?" sobbed the other Abe as he cradled his hand.

"Why won't you be better?" Abe snapped back, pushing the other Abe off and getting groggily to his feet. He was already exhausted, and he hadn't even thrown a punch yet, he was in no physical shape to be brawling, but the doppelganger Abe was just as bad.

"I can't let you be you, not anymore. We have to be better. These islands deserve better, and if that means I have to defeat you, then that's what I'm going to do."

He swung a fist. An inexpert haymaker and surprisingly nailed the other Abe across the jaw, a satisfying crunch echoed down the corridor. His hand throbbed with pain, he felt as if he may have broken the bones in his hand.

Abe clinched his throbbing hand, just as the other Abe made an advanced swing to his gut, blood dripping from his split lip.

"You... should... stay... down," doppelganger Abe connected each punch, segmenting each word with thumping wallops to Abe's gut.

Abe crumpled to his knees and puked all over his suit; a throat-burning mixture of green bile and the chimichanga he'd had for lunch. The other Abe kicked at his side, sending him crashing to the ground in a foetal position.

"These are my islands now, Abe. You should have been me ages ago, but you were too pussy. You allowed the Moon in, you let it be on our turf, well, no more! I'm gonna beat the Moon, and then I'm gonna be mayor; a better mayor than you ever were. I'm gonna rip these islands to shreds and be king of all the ashes. And no one is gonna stop me," he snarled.

He turned, and limped from the debate hall, into the Gyre's evening air.

Amendment 14

The rights of citizens of the Gyre to vote in elections shall not be denied or abridged by the Gyre by reason or failure of said citizen to be alive. However, the Gyre does take this opportunity to rule out evil clones from voting. It's one citizen, one right to vote, people. Seriously, stop with the multiple facsimiles to gain extra votes.

Everything hurt. His ribs, his hand, his arms, his guts, his face, his pride. Abe wasn't quite sure what was the worst part, the physical hurt, nausea, or the fact he'd gotten his ass handed to him by... well, himself? He really should have been able to at least get a draw out of it.

He groaned on the floor and tried not to throw up again. Perhaps he could stay here, beaten and defeated? Maybe that was best? Maybe the other Abe was just what the Gyre needed? A monstrous Abe to defeat the Moon—the enemy of my enemy is my friend, kind of thing?

Except, that was total pig shit. The other Abe would be just as bad, if not worse, for the Gyre than the Moon ever could be. It would be hookers, and lies, and sex and money and power and more lies forever. He'd be a king of shit, turning everything to garbage. Abe knew his own dark self, and it would be a dictator if he let it. If he gave up and didn't defeat himself, there would be nothing left to call the Gyre.

He pulled himself up to a knock-kneed wobble and started out after the doppelganger. The evening sun was turning the sky to a blazing-orange, and the gulls cawed out over the rising tide. Ahead, the other Abe was walking gingerly down the sidewalk. It looked as though his crotch injury was still taking its toll on him.

"Hey!" panted Abe, "We haven't finished, yet!"

The other Abe turned, exasperation contorting his face. Painfully, he hobbled away at a slightly faster pace.

Abe was holding his side, his ribs throbbing from the kick to his guts. Every step hurt, every breath burned, but he edged in closer gritting his teeth, closing the gap between himself and his other self.

As the doppelganger ducked into an alleyway, Abe caught up with him, grabbed hold of his shoulder and spun him around. Abe expected his right hook would miss him, but he took the blow to the top of his head, rather than his temple. It still hurt but didn't cause him to blackout.

Abe really wasn't sure with his fighting skills, never mind the close quarter action. It was not a moment he'd ever mentally rehearsed. His right hand still ached from the earlier impact, so he decided to go for a surprise left. His southpaw skill attempt ended more with a slap, than a punch. Awkwardly, his hand skimmed over the doppelganger's face, smearing snot and spit into the creases of his palm.

"Get off!"

The pair scuffled, clumsily patting at each other until the whole thing just became one inelegant wrestling match. Abe managed to get his arm wrapped around his doppelganger's neck and shoulder, bending him double in a haphazard headlock.

He was worriedly pondering the next move, which was always a mistake in a fight, when the other Abe made a move instead. Pushing with all his weight, he shoved the pair of them over, and they both tumbled into the canal.

Abe hit the freezing water, and immediately swallowed a mouthful of salt and garbage. The water's slime clung to him. The world had turned in crazy directions, and he wasn't sure which way was up. Already the breath in his lungs was brittle and stale. He kicked in a random direction, but that didn't appear to help, get him closer to the shore.

His chest was a lump of burning hot coal, and his heartbeat was a cacophony of throbbing noises drumming around inside his head. The grey water, and the swirls of garbage made vision impossible to see the surface of the water.

A few bubbles escaped from his nostrils, and he quickly used them as surfaces beacons.

He crashed through the scum layer of flotsam, gasping at the air and coughing violently. The flotsam was calm at the moment, no undercurrent tugged him farther from the canal. He bobbed and pushed his way through the disgusting water to a set of steps which lead back up to the alleyway where he'd been fighting. He hauled himself up onto the first stone step, and his arms gave out from exhaustion.

He sprawled out over the bottom step, trying to catch his breath, resting his cheek on the cool stone step. He noticed the doppelganger Abe splashing around. It grabbed at his ankle and pinned his leg down. Abe tried to shake it off, but his weak attempt did nothing. Another hand grabbed hold of his calf and used it for leverage to climb out of the water.

"God, that was tiring." Abe thought.

They both lay panting deeply, covered in plastic six-pack holders, discarded cardboard, and used tissues, with their pockets full of crab shit and foam from the seawater. Almost inexorably, the other Abe looked over then swung his fist down onto Abe's unguarded chest.

"Why won't you just die?" doppelganger Abe panted.

Abe couldn't answer. There was something inside him, some last vestige of decency that just would not let this baser version of himself loose on the Gyre.

Another exhausted strike, then another and another pounding over Abe's chest.

"Come on die, already. Die and leave these islands to me, I want them!"

With every humping blow, Abe realised how bored he was of this fight, how bored he was of this version of himself fighting to rule. How pathetic the other Abe really was, how needy he was, how childish.

Abe felt a burst of energy, something; maybe his thoughts made him feel stronger. He pushed himself to his knees, as the other Abe tried to scratch his face like an alley cat.

Its fingers bent backwards, folding like paper over Abe's flesh, unable to break his skin. A shocked look fell across the doppelganger's face and miraculously the doppelganger began to turn to mush.

Abe realised that this version of him... It was nothing, it was like a piece of cut out paper.

He dug his fingernails deep into the doppelganger's face, clawed at his flesh. Abe noticed his skin peeled off and sounded like ripping loose-leaf paper. A sliver of the other Abe's face dangled from the tips of his fingernails. Abe examined the strip of flesh, and oddly the skin was fleshy-colored on one side, opposed to other side having a small typeset printed across the flesh, just like a newspaper.

With the strength of something real versus something imaginary, Abe bodily picked up his doppelganger.

"What are you... how?" squealed the doppelganger.

Abe didn't answer this thing, this wretched, pixie magical version of himself that he no longer wanted to be.

"Put me down! You don't have to do this! We... we can still be friends, right?" babbled the doppelganger as Abe moved him over to the water.

He lowered the other Abe to the water, holding him by the lapels of his ruined, sewage-stained suit.

"I'll give you anything, anything at all. Name it, it's yours."

Abe dropped the doppelganger over the edge and pushed its head into the flotsam. The struggling attempt was useless, this thing was not real anymore; just a piece of newsprint inked with yesterday's headlines.

The doppelganger's eyes went wide as colors started to bleed off his face. The lapels of his jacket felt mushy in Abe's hands. The doppelganger disintegrated into mush and pulp. The last thing Abe saw, reflecting in the white froth and foam, was his own fake eyes pleading and the silent scream from beneath the garbage.

Amendment 15

The Gyre deems it proper for all citizens to always examine their origins and memories. It is only by examining our past in great detail that we can hope to forge our future. The Gyre also deems it proper for all citizens to always have one eye on their future. For, if we do not pay attention to our destination, we are unlikely to get there. Citizens are not advised to pay any attention to the present, as it has only recently been the future (and should have been paid attention too then) and will soon be the past (and can be examined at their leisure then.)

Abraham Lincoln, prospective mayoral candidate, had returned to the debate hall. His clothes were soaked and covered in garbage. A plastic six-pack beer holder formed a bracelet around his wrist, and his pockets filled with crab shit, dripping an oily substance down the length of his pants. His hair was bedraggled, and pieces of seaweed literally strewn within it. He wasn't certain, but he was sure that he had a black eye and a split lip to boot, but he hadn't dared look in a mirror.

There wasn't time to do anything about his appearance. Besides, after fighting himself, it would feel wrong to try and hide behind an image again. He'd just have to face the electorate as he was.

On the stage, The Stones were rocking. The lights were low as the band kicked out a medley of *Jumpin' Jack Flash, Brown Sugar* and *Like A Rolling Stone*. Mick Jagger was in a full cockerel strut, parading around the small stage as the Gyre's folk trundled in.

"How would you feel? To be on your own, like a complete unknown, no direction home, just like a rolling stone," howled Jagger at the uncaring audience. The cover was a bold choice but perhaps a bit on the nose.

Abe cautiously poked his head out from the corner of the curtain, scanning the audience for friendly faces. There were some he recognized.

The journalist, Caroline, sat in the front row. She held in her hand a wand with a bright ribbon attached which she flicked and swirled. Abe assumed this was her new way of trying to express her article about him. It looked like some sort of ribbon gymnastic thing? He wasn't sure.

The bear sat next to her, squished onto one of the small, wooden, fold-away chairs, which were set out for the debate. He stared glumly up at the stage.

"If you ain't got nothing, then you got nothing to lose," sang Jagger, sweat pouring down from his mop of brown hair.

"There's always more to lose, ignoramus," the bear signed. "Everything is a downward spiral of loss, until eventual oblivion."

"How would you feel?" screeched Jagger, "To be on your own, like a complete unknown, no direction home, just like a rolling stone?"

Silently the bear signed, "It feels like I'm screaming for redemption at a pile of children's bones."

Above, sat on the townhall's supporting rafter beams, the fairy-folk swung and gesticulated, fucked and blew raspberries at everything and everyone.

The final rattling chords from the medley bounced and stormed around the room. The audience politely applauded from their seats: no one stood, no one whooped.

"Fuck you, you old, scraggly, scrotum!" shouted a green-skinned pixie.

"Thank you, thank you very much," Jagger chanted. Abe had no doubt that Jagger was polite about the lukewarm applause because of the enormous paycheck he was receiving after his performance.

"We've just got one more song for you bastards!" shouted Keith Richards, a cigarette dangling from his lower lip, his skin cracking and warping as he spoke. "...And then, we'll introduce some politician asshole or other."

"Yeah, we've been asked to play this song, especially for your favourite candidate, or something? I dunno, some hedgehog wrote us a letter about it. And we thought, fuck it. Hit it!" said Jagger.

A familiar riff, which Abe knew well, rang out over the slightly bored audience.

"We get it on almost every night. When that moon is huge and bright. That's a phantasmagorical delight, everybody's rocking in the moonlight."

He saw the crowd sway in time to the hypnotic rhythm. Aimlessly, the audience mouthed the words along to the song with eyes blank and glassy.

"Everybody here and that's alright, they don't bark but sure do bite. They keep things loose, they keep it light, everybody's rocking in the moonlight!"

Drool dripped from slack jaws in the audience. Even the bear was transfixed by the hypnotizing music.

Abe's brain was fuzzy, as his memories dragged him to when he'd arrived. He'd washed up on the hard side of the Gyre, in one of the outer islands, where people drank distilled rock-pool water because it was cheap and plentiful. He could taste that salty fish-brew coating his teeth and tongue even now. And the taste of limpet stew, the first thing he'd eaten on the islands.

Everyone was an immigrant to the Gyre, everyone washed up, and Abe was just the same. He'd come ashore, ragged and coughing, covered in garbage, and the islands had welcomed him, giving him free food and free drink and a place to sleep.

Then, the old in the bone, grade A-bastard instincts had kicked in, and he'd started his relentless politicking to the top. He'd monetised the washed-up immigrant welcome package. When you got ashore, you were greeted with a bowl of limpet broth and a glass of rock-pool water, and you didn't pay then, it was all charged to your account within the Gyre. And that kind of pure-bred son-of-a-bitchery was the kind of thinking that got you noticed in powerful circles.

In the cool of the moonlit June nights, he'd made deals on the dockside. Arrangements that would take him all the way to the Mayoral office.

Everyone owed him something, and he owed everyone something back. It was how life worked. The recycling plant, the ice cream parlor, the Snowmen. The bloody Snowmen! He was up to his eyeballs in debt with Mr. Frosty.

He still didn't really know what Mr. Frosty's angle was. He'd been backed by the Snowmen again, and that little arrangement would almost certainly cost him dearly, they might be unhappy with the new and improved un-bastard Abe. But, as was life, he was always in hock to someone or another.

But what was Mr. Frosty's end game? He doubted it was to get the ice cream parlor built.

The music swirled, and Abe noticed his own soaked feet were tapping. He was fucking tapping along to his enemy's theme tune! What was going on?

The music seemed to permeate into him, filling his veins with the electric blue fire of wanting to conform; be like everyone else, sing, move your feet, consume the music, let the music own you. Dance in the moonlight, just like everyone else. The future is bright, like the moon's face. That harvest moon.

The only beings not affected were the fairy-folk. They continued to swing on the rafters or defecate on the townsfolk below.

"It's all fucking bollocks, and you're all cum-guzzling twats!" shouted a green pixie.

"Sleepy, sleepy. They's all asleepy!" cackled a pink-skinned one.

"Rocking in the moonlight, everybody's feeling warm and right, it's such a fine and natural sight, everybody's rocking in the moonlight," The Rolling Stones sang together.

"And now, would you please welcome to the stage, your mayoral candidate, The Moon!" Jagger yelled.

The Moon rolled out onto the stage as the band repeated the chorus, the audience joining in.

"Rocking in the moonlight, everybody's feeling warm and right, it's such a fine and natural sight, everybody's rocking in the moonlight."

Abe was horrified to see the journalist and the bear whoop and cheer as The Moon rolled center stage and took a bow. His heart sank. Even they were affected. What was this strange pull The Moon had on everyone?

The Stones finished their song in a final ear cracking crescendo. Keith threw his guitar onto the floor. The guitar burst into flaming ravens, which took flight, cawing their way up into the rafters. The audience whooped and cheered, at the spectacular ending.

"Fuck off, Ravenses!" screamed the green-skinned pixie, as the birds came closer. The fairy-folk scattered, flying to safety, or simply vanishing into nothingness with a loud 'pop'. The ravens cawed and screamed their way out of open windows into the dark night.

The Stones moved to the back of the stage, giving room for Abe's band to waddle on.

The four crabs clawed their way to the center stage. One got behind a small drum set, another a double bass. The third pressed its mandibles to the kazoo. The fourth just stood at the back and raised its pincers.

The drummer began, one, two, three, four.

The bass player took it up, and the kazoo did his best to blow out *You Are My Sunshine*... But mandibles and kazoos did not go hand-and-hand; or in this case claw-and-claw. The fourth crab remained stoically silent; pincers raised.

Please don't take my sunshine away, the crab buzzed into the kazoo.

The crab playing the kazoo scuttled aside and allowed the fourth crab to be the spotlight. The drum and double bass carried on at the same pace as the fourth crab shuffled forward. It snapped its pincers and stamped its claws, like a Spanish castanet dancer, to the beat... *You Are My Sunshine*.

There were extra flourishes, along the lines of an impromptu tap routine. Click-click-click, cliiiick, cliiiick, click-click-click cliiiick, cliiiick (clickity-click-click). Click-click-click cliiick, cliiick, click-click-click cliiiiiiiiick (clickety-click-click)

Abe pondered over the fact: crabs really do have small brains.

The torturous music was ended by the kazoo crab blowing an ear-splittingly high, *please don't take my sunshine away,* and then a flat sounding fanfare.

Abe straightened his soggy jacket and strode out onto the stage. He waved his hands, but no one was applauding. The audience sat in stunned silence.

"Wooo! Great job, guys. Great job!" he said into his podium mic. He smiled and stuck a thumb up to the crabs. They all got out their Lincoln flags and waved them enthusiastically. Those were four votes he could probably count on. The only four.

The audience looked at him in horror, his bedraggled hair, his soaked suit, the crab shit in his pockets.

Really doubling down on that crab vote, aren't you Abe? He thought.

"Well, folks, I think you'll agree that was some mighty fine music. Firstly, a big hand for The Rolling Stones!" Abe applauded, and so did the crowd, with wild abandon. "And secondly, from The Crab Four." He clapped again, this time on his own.

The four crabs lifted up a cardboard sign which read: EQUAL RIGHTS FOR SNOWMEN!

The smile froze on Abe's face as it all clicked into place.

Oh, shit, he thought. T*hat's the game, is it? Being pushed for equal rights for Snowmen? That's really subtle, Frosty.*

"That's fabulous, boys. Well done. Ladies and Gentlemen, The Crab Four, aren't they wonderful?"

Two confetti cannons went off on the stage's corners, showering both The Moon and Abe in bright slivers of paper.

Offstage, there was a squeaking winch and Master of Ceremonies, Bernadette, descended from the fly system. Her dead body hung ungainly from a thick bit of hemp rope as two burly sea otters sweated and barked in the wings as they lowered her.

She wore a dark top hat, a red velvet ring master's jacket, black fishnet tights and thigh-length leather boots. She held a microphone in one hand and a pained expression on her face.

"'Ere, bumface, that's ain't no flying!" said the green pixie, taking wing to demonstrate the correct method of flying.

The dead woman landed, with a clonk, on the stage and the two sweating sea otter-stagehands came on and bit the rope free. She raised her microphone to her dead lips.

"Good evening, Ladies and Gentlemen," she growled. "I am Master of Ceremonies for tonight's debate between Abe Lincoln and Mayor Moon."

Abe gritted his teeth. He was still the mayor, not this upstart lunar body, but he held back. Attacking the MC would do him no good.

The crowd applauded.

"First," continued Bernadette, cracking her whip for silence, "I invite Mayor Moon to open debate. Ladies, Gentlemen, animals, dead people, dinosaurs and chewing gum, I give you Mayor Moon."

Amendment 16

> *The Gyre deems it necessary to point out that the Master of Ceremonies word is law during an election. Should the Master of Ceremonies declare war, then war is declared. War may only be declared on real things, states or towns. Unreal states, towns or people may not have war declared on them, as they don't exist.*

The Moon rolled up to its speaking podium. Its regolith exterior made a hard grinding noise on the pine stage, like a bowling ball travelling down an alley. Caroline couldn't see any mouth on the lunar body. Her wrist ached from the constant swirling and popping of the ribbon thing; she stopped waving it around and thought. How was the Moon planning on giving a speech and then participate in a question-and-answer session?

From one side of the stage, a spindly, six-foot-tall figure appeared. Caroline's eyes wanted to slide right past it as if her brain couldn't cope with its presence, but it was just too 'there' to be ignored. It was grey and hairless, with black, almond-shaped eyes and on its bulbous head, it had a scar the shape of a question mark.

"Shit, it's one of them grey fuckers!" shouted a pixie, from the rafters.

"Yeah, and they smell like rocket fuel and vomit," said another pixie.

It stepped down from the stage and passed a few of people in the audience, then stopped in front of a random member. The man looked shocked. The thing that couldn't be there reached behind its back, it pulled out a metal cylinder, and aimed a blue flashing light at the man, he disintegrated with a scream.

Fear shot through Caroline, she wanted to run, get away from this obvious monster, but she was frozen in place.

That couldn't have happened, things like this creature did not exist. People did not get vaporized right before your eyes.

The spindly figure reached down into the dust pile and pulled out a singed tongue and the man's scalp complete with wafts of smoking hair. The spindly thing opened its mouth to a great yawning pink chasm; the stink of rotting seagull intestines filtered through the air. The figure jammed the singed tongue into its open maw, then clicked its teeth together twice.

"Ladies and Gentlemen," it said, in a raspy voice full of graveyard dust as it returned to the lectern. "I am the voice of The Moon. It is I who will speak for The Moon throughout this debate. You will remember my words. You will not remember me, because creatures like me do not exist."

It pulled the scalp of the man over its bald head and smoothed back its new blonde locks.

The words made sense to Caroline; spindly, alien figures, like the one talking, did not exist. Therefore, this one in front of her couldn't really be there.

"We believe that the office of the mayor should be given to The Moon. Our opponent, Abraham Lincoln," the figure turned its bulbous head and stared at Abe, "is nothing but a philanderer. A money-grubbing, power-hungry, toad of a human. He does nothing but line his own pockets with wealth and power. He is for the privileged, he is not for hard-working people, like you or I, or Mayor Moon. He does not even respect you enough to turn up today in a clean suit. Instead, he comes in smelling of garbage and crab shit!"

"He's right about that!" a man shouted from the crowd.

"Abe threw a baby in a fire, and he didn't get arrested or nothing!" said a woman.

There was a general murmur of agreement. The voice of The Moon returned its gaze to the audience. Using its thin-fingered hand, it continued to try and smooth out the stolen scalp over its oddly round head.

"Mayor Moon understands you. Mayor Moon loves you. He has watched over you for aeons. Now, let him help you." The voice of The Moon raised its arms and outstretched them to grasp the audience. "Give your lives over to Mayor Moon, and he will look after you. Just as he has always looked after you...remember."

The voice was a honey drop in Caroline's ears. Her memory skipped, to a time in a blue field. A boy had taken her there, and she'd lost her virginity that night, beneath the moon's cold gaze. What was that boy's name? Johnny? Jimmy? Jimmothy? She couldn't remember.

What color had his eyes been? White? Purple? Octavian? Again, she couldn't remember. All the while the moon had been there, above them, watching like a voyeur.

The moon. The Moon. Great globus Moon. Watching. Waiting. Loving with them. Knowing what was best. Seeing into everyone's heart.

The voice of the Moon had finished his opening speech, and Abe was now given time at the microphone.

"I want to thank all you folks for coming out tonight to this debate. That was quite some opening statement given there by my opponent, The Moon. Man, I just can't get over that. The Moon. And as he was saying, he's always been around. So, my question is, if he's always been around, how come he ain't done nothing?"

The question stirred an uprise of mumbling from the crowd.

"Me? Well, I've been mayor. I've worked hard for the Gyre—yes, some of you may scoff at that. I am of the Gyre, just look at me, I'm covered in the Gyre's juices now. You can't accuse me of sitting up in the sky and just watching you. I can't help but think that's just a bit creepy. And really, what do any of us know about The Moon? Do we know its history? You all know mine; it was splashed over all the papers the other day. But The Moon? Nah, don't know nothing about it. And that's why you should vote for me; I am the known quantity."

There was a small smattering of applause. No one was sure if that was for what Abe had said, or because he had finished.

"Thank you for those opening speeches," growled the zombie. "Now, on to question one. Beginning with you Mr. Lincoln, why are you the best choice for prosperity within the Gyre?"

"I think the central question for this election is, what kind of country do we want to be, and who do we trust to be in charge of that future?" said Abe, squishing as he pulled himself up to his full height.

"Firstly, we have to build an economy that works for everyone; men and women, animals and dinosaurs, zombies, chewing gum, everyone. That means good jobs, new jobs, like jobs at the ice cream parlor. I want to make the economy fairer, starting with a guarantee for equal pay to all, whether you're a man, a woman, a zombie or even a crab."

The raspy sound of a kazoo played a familiar fanfare, followed by the click-click-click of pincers. The crabs rousing applause verses everyone else's mumbled disbelief.

"How many years has he promised that ice cream parlor?" yelled a man from the crowd.

"I don't wanna get paid the same as no dirty crab!" an older woman proclaimed.

"Thank you, Mr. Lincoln," said Bernadette, moving on before the crowd got ugly. "And now you, Mayor Moon, what makes you the perfect candidate to bring prosperity to the Gyre?"

"The Moon will allow everyone to keep all the diamonds they currently have," said The Voice of the Moon matter-of-factly. "The Moon will also reduce taxes for the big employers, they, in turn, will pass this saving on to you. They will not keep any of this extra money."

There was murmuring of "Hey, that kind of makes sense," from somewhere in the crowd. A few roars from the dinosaurs, sounded from the crowd, claiming their understanding.

"This is what you should have been doing for years," said The Voice of the Moon, pointing an accusing finger at Abe. "Not promising a new ice cream parlor every election, and then stealing the money."

Abe coughed audibly. "I...I never..." he started.

"On to question two," snapped Bernadette. "This random question from the audience. It goes, what is the opposite of a koala? Mayor Moon, you are first."

The Voice of the Moon pondered for a moment, stroking its chin with its long, thin fingers. "A koala is a chlamydia ridden animal," it said, finally, "much like Abe here, who has had numerous sexual partners."

"Hey!" protested Abe, but The Voice of the Moon went on.

"So, the opposite of that would be Mayor Moon, who has had no scandals, sexual or otherwise, since it has taken office."

There was a general smattering of applause at the quick and pithy answer.

"Mr. Lincoln, your random question is, what fictional character do you have the hots for?"

"Why does it always come back to sex for me?" Abe asked in exasperation.

"I don't know, but it always seems to," heckled an audience member. Laughter rattled around the crowd, and Caroline saw the blood drain from Abe's face.

"It's not going well," signed the Bear next to her. "It does not matter really, the universe is just a meaningless eternity, there is no god, no justice, no point to any of it. It all adds up to nothing, and we're all going to die. There will be no reward for anything we have done or haven't done."

She saw his tattoos, beneath his fur. His beautiful tattoos and thick hair, loaded with musk and promise. And his great heart that was so full of worry about the future.

She wanted to show him, to comfort him, and tell him not to worry, that it would all work out in the end. She wanted to say that he was right and wrong at the same time, that yes, their time on earth was fleeting, but that didn't make it pointless. There was still beauty in a moment, even if there was no ultimate point. That may be, that was the point?

Softly, just on the edge of hearing, there was a clap-clap-clapping. The air around the town hall crackled with electric green fire.

"Peoples, the oysters are close, we now enter the quick-fire round of questions. Mayor Moon, how will you deal with divides between humans, zombies, animals, dinosaurs and chewing gum in our society?"

"If you vote for it, everyone will be happy under Mayor Moon. No one will be left behind. Everyone will be rich. Mayor Moon will shine down his love upon everyone."

The clapping grew louder, more real somehow. It clacked around the whole room, emanating from the air itself.

"Mr. Lincoln, how decisive or indecisive are you?" said the zombie.

"Hey! How come he gets a proper one, and I get a random one?"

"Is that your answer?"

"Ummmmmmmmmm," said Abe.

"That will count," said the zombie in finality. "Mayor Moon, what game do you wish you could act out in real life?"

"Armageddon," snapped The Voice of the Moon. Then it added as an afterthought, "on every other nation in the world."

There was once again applause, this time more fervent. Some even whistled and whooped their approval.

"Yeah, stick it to them other nations!"

"Mr. Lincoln," continued Bernadette, in a gabbling pace. "What happened to all the money that should have gone to build the ice cream parlor over the last eight years?"

"Aaaaah," said Abe, turning a sickly color.

The electric green fire buzzed and spun its way across every surface, clustering to form glowing patches. The oysters shifted into this reality, forming damp patches and clumps all over the hall, on chairs, in corners, strung along the wooden rafters, everywhere. They opened and closed rhythmically, exposing their bright pink inner flesh, sucking in tiny airborne krill to feed on.

Bernadette held up her hands before Abe could get any further in whatever bullshit answer he was going to cook up.

"Peoples, that is end of debate. Oysters have returned, and voting must now begin."

"But...but," Abe stuttered. "I haven't put my case forward yet."

The dead woman turned her pale, lifeless eyes to Abe. A worm erupted from her cheek and dropped to the floor.

"Oysters are here, Mr. Lincoln. The debate ends now—it is the rules," intoned the Master of Ceremonies, with the finality of a closed tomb. She produced a giant gavel from her coat's pocket and banged it on her thigh-high boot's sole.

"The Moon is not even a citizen of the Gyre. Therefore, he is ineligible to hold office!" cried Abe.

"Wait!" growled the Master of Ceremonies, holding up a pale, dead hand for silence from the crowd. "These serious allegations. Mayor Moon, what you have to say about this?"

The Moon rotated softly. The voice of The Moon spoke up, in its dry and dusty voice.

"The Moon has always been. The Moon will always be. It has hung over the Gyre for aeons, just as it has hung over other places. The Moon is of all places. It claims the right to be your mayor, as you, Abraham Lincoln, have abandoned it. Every one of you, in the Gyre, are all castaways, you all wash up here; the Moon is no different. It just wants to be one of you and serve."

The Moon rolled forward slightly, in a nod.

There was a stunned silence, and then a single clap-clap-clap, as one person got to their feet. Then another got to their feet. Then another, and another, and another, until the whole room was on its feet with a thunderous applause.

"Very well," said the Master of Ceremonies, in her gravel voice. "It's time for the voting to begin!"

Amendment 17

Time travelling, pan-dimensional whore houses are not real things and therefore shall be considered illegal within the Gyre. Citizens may frequent these brothels, under the assumption that whatever goes on inside the brothel does so in another version of reality. Since other versions of reality do not exist, no crime can have been committed therein. Time travelling, pan-dimensional brothels (which do not exist) must clearly display a figure from literature as a mascot, to show that they are not real things.

As one tribe, the humans of the Gyre lined up to cast their votes. The zombies lined up next to them, as they were nearly as good as the humans and were therefore allowed to vote directly after them. The animals and dinosaurs were shuffled to the back, being of a lesser race but still voters. The chewing gum clung to the humans' shoes because chewing gum always went that way.

Abe stared, hollow-eyed, down at his lectern, dripping an oily substance and garbage water into puddles at his feet. The debate had not gone according to plan, it hadn't even gone according to nightmare. And all around, the oysters clapped in mock applause.

His plans for the ice cream parlor development complex, gone. His love of being mayor, defeated. His love for the town, even though he often stole money from it, ruined. Deep down he loved the Gyre. He loved its washed-up nature, its willingness to recycle the old and make new, it's horribly gullible people who were rubbish at doing their accounts. He loved it all. And now, it was being taken away from him. He'd tried to please everyone and ended up satisfying no one.

He'd even defeated his old self, his loathsome, philandering, sexualising self. But he hadn't had a chance to show off the new him, to show the people of the Gyre that he had changed and could be a better mayor. Perhaps five minutes of reform were not really enough to make up for a lifetime of scamming?

Now, there was nothing left, and the votes were being cast.

The peoples shuffling into the voting booth would punch the parrot who represented their chosen candidate. Abe's parrot sounded very lively and distinctly unmolested. There was barely a squawk from The Moon's parrot, blood was leaking on the floor from its side of the booth.

"Gwwwaaaark, Polly is lonely!" shouted Abe's parrot.

"Mwerk! Mercy!" came the feeble voice of the other. "Bluey's not well, Weeeewooooo! Mwerk! Tasting blood!"

Abe wanted to curl up inside himself and stay there forever, because it was over. He was finished, he'd lost.

The Voice of The Moon was what they would remember, its glib answers and his fluffed ones too.

Punch after punch landed on The Moon's parrot, and his parrot squawked merrily away, totally unharmed.

"Gwwwwwark! Polly is unloved! Gwwwwwwark!"

Abe needed to get out of this hall as the future cemented around him, a hard, brutal future where he would not be mayor anymore, a future where he had no voice, a future he didn't want to be a part of.

He could feel the tears welling up, it wasn't fair, it wasn't right. He wanted his right to speak, to be heard, but he had missed his chance. And now, no one would listen, he was yesterday's man: disenfranchised, just like the Snowmen or the Pixies.

This was humiliating. There wasn't even any squawking coming from The Moon's parrot anymore, just dull wheezing.

He watched as the crabs scuttled into the voting booth. The last one through the curtain looked up at Abe and gave him a pincers-up. Stupid crabs, they never knew when they were beaten.

"Gaawwwwwwaaarrrrrkkkkk! Polly got pinched! Gwark!" exclaimed Abe's parrot.

"I think this parrot might be dead," came a voice from the other booth, "Do we need a new one?"

It was already a landslide. Abe had to leave, there was no point in even being in here. With his brow furrowed, his lips pursed and his shoes still dripping oily, garbage, he stepped down from the stage.

The oysters clapped and stuck out their feeding gills, like thick pink tongues. The crabs tried to scuttle after him, but he ran off too fast for their tiny articulated legs to keep up with him.

He slammed his hands into the doors and pushed them open, striding out into the cold autumnal air. There was a haze of sea-spray drifting, and Abe couldn't tell if he was crying or not as it condensed on his cheeks. The street-river sloshed along, slewing the recycling down to the plant.

He hurt inside, and he was afraid. He was afraid of a future which didn't need the old him anymore and didn't know about the reformed him. The Gyre had rejected him as mayor. Even so, there were places he knew, which would always welcome the old him. There were places where, for a time and a fee, he could be wanted again.

The red-fronted cat house was never far away when you wanted it. On the front, it had a pair of large eyes and a huge grin of a black-and-white Cheshire Cat advertisement, displaying hoarding. Its mouth opening and closing as a gargled and crusty recording shouted out, "Whores Whores! Whores! The best whores in town!"

The doorbell was shaped like a clitoris. Abe leaned forward, extended his tongue, and licked. The vaginal doors parted slightly, with a wet smacking sound. He squeezed through, feeling the heat and warmth and wetness soak through his jacket.

He emerged, covered in secretions, which was an improvement on the oil garbage he had been covered in. The first thing he always noticed was the dryness of the air. The Gyre's air was permanently damp, but the whore house always felt dry, probably because it was in another dimension. A sweet smell of hyacinth, forget-me-not and crepe suzette wafted over the air. The lobby rang with the sounds of fornication and Mick Hucknall singing Simply Red's greatest hits.

He stalked to the reception. The headless receptionist turned her neck hole to face him.

"Aaaan iiiuugggg eeeeellllgggggghhhh ooooooo?" asked the receptionist, spattering him with throat phlegm.

"Get me a whore," he growled. "And get us a bottle of whiskey, a tin of peppermint jam, an egg whisk and a flying helmet. I feel like I wanna do some shit."

He threw a credit card at the girl and waited for her to feel the embossed name and inhale the rich, pomade edging.

"Iiiiggchhhhtt aaahaaaaay, eeeeeerrrrrrrr," she said. "Iiiiiixxxxxeeeee iiiiizzzzzzz eeeeeeeee. Oooooooomnnnnn iiiinnnnnnnneeeeeeennnnnn."

Abe took the key, labelled room 19, and thanked the girl. She was a pretty little thing. Her neck stump was beautifully etched with blackened veins, and raw redish meat dangling at its edges.

He trudged up the stairs, disgusted at himself. He was doing it again, why did he do it to himself? Nevertheless, he wanted to feel shitty. He wanted to be a shit. The world was a cesspool, and he just wanted to dive right in and wallow in its filth.

He found room 19 and placed the key in the lock. He knew this was a mistake. Sex was his downfall, but in the end, what the hell? He'd tried to deny who he was. He'd tried to flim-flam the audience. He'd tried to outshine The Moon. In the end, he hadn't stood a chance, so why not be who he really was?

The girl, Trixie, splayed across on the bed. Her skin was a ghostly pale shade, probably from the blood loss, with a white fuzz of hair covering her body. Her neck hole glubbed and sucked at the air. Abe felt himself harden.

She opened her arms and accepted him in his wretchedness. She recognized who he was. Abe the fucker. Abe the shit. Abe the philanderer. Abe the user. Finally, he was where he belonged, if only for a time.

Amendment 18

> *Citizens of the Gyre shall vote by means of punching a parrot. Humans may punch once with either hand. Zombies may only punch with their most reliable hand, as they have unnatural strength. Animals and Dinosaurs may only punch with one paw or hoof. Chewing gum may not punch, as it has no hands, but may indicate, as it sees fit, on which parrot it would punch if it could. The candidate whose parrot receives the most punches will be declared the winner by the Master of Ceremonies. The winning candidate will, at that moment, take up their responsibilities and have the power of law on their side.*

The bear sullenly plodded on another step as the queue of animals made their way into the voting booth. It all seemed remarkably pointless, but he was in the line, and it also seemed pointless not to vote.

There was still a buzzing in his brain. A tiny voice, saying to give up, give in, just float along. The voice comforted him, making it was much easier to relinquish that responsibility. He would vote because that was a legal thing, but why vote against The Moon? The Moon was a friend, it understood the pointlessness, and it wanted to take away the responsibility. If nothing mattered, then why should the bear care?

The four crabs scuttled in front of him, clicking their pincers and raising them high above their heads. He watched them dolefully and wished he too could be so gullible. Stupid crabs, always optimistic.

Abe had abandoned his podium, in some sort of shock state. The bear didn't blame him, the total existential anguish of the universe meaning nothing was enough to drive anyone into a shocked state. He was surprised that the utter futility of every endeavour had only just occurred to Abe.

Caroline was behind him, blindly tapping him with her gymnastic ribbon. She too had a dreamy look in her eyes. It was odd that she was behind him. Usually, humans went first, but Caroline had been insistent, stubbornly grabbing hold of his arm and not letting go when she'd been ushered forward.

The bear's brain felt even fuzzier as they passed; The Voice of The Moon standing by his podium humming in a low melodic tune. The sound surrounded him, confirming that he should just give up—everything was pointless.

He shuffled to the voting booth, lifting the red velvet curtain, and went inside. The cabin was small, and the light which filtered in from outside; was stained cherry by the velvet curtain. The two parrots were at the tent's rear, the first one sat on a hip-high, ring perch and looked largely unmolested.

"Polly is utterly fine! Gwwwwaaaarrrrkkkk!" squawked the parrot.

At the foot of another hip-high, ring perch was a heap of blood and feathers. Most of the parrot's feathers had been ripped from its body exposing its pale pimpled flesh, blackened, and bruised. One of its eyes was swollen shut, the other eye leaked a milky-white liquid. Blood oozed from the parrot's beak and anus as it gurgled, unhappily on the floor.

The bear needed to choose. Abe's parrot sat, staring wide-eyed at him. Abe stood for... Well, what did he stand for? The bear couldn't remember. There was a vague itch in the back of his brain, something about The Moon being evil? It also had something to do with the pixies? He tried to grab at the memory, but it slipped away, and the dancing siren Voice of The Moon seeped back into his brain.

The Moon loves you. The Moon only wants what's best for you. A vote for The Moon is a vote for freedoms.

But what did he care about freedoms? Freedom was an illusion and pointless. You couldn't be free when the destiny of the universe was prefixed, and it would all end in death. What freedom was there?

The Moon will drop taxes for you, allowing you to keep more of your hard-earned money.

But the bear didn't care about money either. Money was just a measurement of how long you could exist in society without producing anything society wanted. Still, since it was all going to end in cold hard oblivion, then the accumulation of time by that method was pointless.

Alright, sang the voice of The Moon, *if it's all pointless, then why not just abdicate responsibility to The Moon? If nothing matters, why not let The Moon make all the decisions?*

The argument was logical. It really didn't matter at all.

His huge paw crunched up into a fist and smashed into the already beaten parrot's rib cage. He heard a cracking of bone, and the parrot wheezed horribly as a greenish sludge came from its beak

He left the polling booth, and his brain cleared almost instantly, like a stiff cold breeze lifting a morning mist. What had he just done? Alright, in the end, it wouldn't matter, but had he really just voted for The Moon?

In a deep part of his mind, he could hear the voice of The Moon laughing.

A few seconds later, Caroline walked out of the voting booth with a puzzled look on her face.

"Did I just...?" she trailed off.

"Vote for The Moon?" he signed. "I think you did. So did I, but I do not know why."

"There was a voice, it told me to do it," said Caroline, rubbing at her temple.

The last of the animals and dinosaurs filed through the voting booth, registering their votes. People, of all types, milled about aimlessly shaking their heads, as if recovering from a stupor, but it was already too late—the vote was done.

The Master of Ceremonies strode forward, her high-heeled boots clicking on the hard wooden floor. She bent down, with a sound of snapping bones and breaking sinews. She tugged, and the curtain came away from the voting booth revealing the result of the election.

"Polly is relatively unscathed. Gwwwwaaarrrrk!" screeched one parrot.

The other parrot was beyond dead.

"I declare that the vote having been ascertained in free and fair manner, that The Moon duly elected Mayor of the Gyre," said the Master of Ceremonies, dropping the curtain on the corpse.

There was a smattering of applause from the groggy crowd.

"Well, that's it then. It doesn't matter anyway," signed the bear.

"Oh, I think it does," said the journalist. "I think it matters a great deal."

From the stage, the Voice of The Moon, the being which couldn't really be there, continued to stand unabashed behind its podium. Its wide mouth broke into a cracked grin, which split across almost the entirety of its face. Its huge almond-shaped eyes shone with glee and malevolence as it rolled back its head and laughed in a thick, dry voice.

The Moon loomed behind it, a giant glowing white ball, casting the Voice of The Moon as a cackling shadow. Then, the Moon's color changed. First, it burned a blazing yellow, then, it blurred a fiery orange, next, a hot pink, and finally, it became a crimson blood.

"Blood Moon," signed the bear.

There was a howling, almost whirring sound coming from outside, it bit at his ears, and his teeth screamed in his gums.

Static-blue electricity sparked along the bear's fur. Lightning bolts spidered from the timber and across the oysters who snapped themselves shut, their applause dying out to a quiet hum.

"Oh, fucking shit-sticks on a brick!" cried one of the pixies. The whole group of fae who'd been watching the voting took wing, scattering in all directions, fleeing from the lightning.

The hall's walls creaked and split, firing giant shards of broken wood into the crowd. The people and animals screamed and brayed as giant splinter-spikes drove through them. An impaled hedgehog lay bleeding on the floor at the bear's feet.

"Social Justice?" it squeaked.

"Your pain is over," he signed. "Embrace the darkness. There is nothing to fear in it. It's just nothing."

He watched as the fire of life died from its eyes.

With a mighty crack, the roof and several pillars of the building broke away. Above, in a whirling maelstrom of roof, wood, crying people and beasts; hovered a gigantic flying saucer.

Caroline's hand slid into the bear's paw. Her small thin fingers clenched tightly to his big soft pad. The bear's heart skipped, and he thought, *this is now, this is happening now.*

Spindly beings stepped forward from the shadows in which they had stood and ignored the event. There were hundreds of them.

The bear and Caroline looked around, panicked at the sudden appearance of things which they had previously ignored. Those beings could not be real, but even as they tried to ignore them, they continued to be there.

A sallow sick feeling burbled in the bear's stomach, as fear gripped him. He wanted to curl into a ball and wait for it all to go away. He wanted to go back, back to before where he only had to worry about the pointlessness of life. This was not some vague, abstract threat of impending doom, this was all very immediate.

The beings raised small metal tubes and fired them into the crowd, disintegrating several people. The spindly figures reached into the dust piles and, just as The Voice of The Moon before them, retrieved teeth and tongues and hair and eyelashes. They began affixing these appendages to themselves, clicking teeth, licking lips, fluttering eyelashes and stroking hair.

"Mankind," they all said in unison, pointing their weapons at the crowd, "you are now ours."

The crowd threw up their hands and surrendered.

Caroline's hand slid out of the bear's grip, and he had never felt so alone as being separated from the journalist. What color were her eyes? He didn't know, but he should—he wanted to. Right now, that was all he wanted to know. He wanted the comfort of his friend.

A black shadow crept over The Moon. It turned, exposing its dark side to the crowd, where the towers and spires dotted it. Gleaming metallic obelisks sparkled and lit up all over the lunar surface. Tiny spacecraft came out of hanger bays all over The Moon, buzzing and swarming like angry evil hornets.

The saucers formed an armada, increasing in size as they flew away from The Moon. First, they were insect size, then, the size of pixies, then birds, then eagles, then small planes. They grew and grew, spinning up into the sky.

The invasion had begun, and the Gyre was doomed.

Epilogue

All citizens of the Gyre must obey The Moon. The Moon is our leader and our friend. His peacekeeping forces love you. If they demand it, lie on the ground, and accept their loving boots on your face. In the event of a death, remember it was probably your own fault.
The Moon loves you.

There was no moon in the sky and there hadn't been for a long time. However, the dark horizon was pockmarked by small, twinkling starlight and grey clouds.

The streets were black, and the houses were unlit, adding an even darker shade against the starlit sky. Yet, small cracks of light still escaped from around the darkened curtains of the sky.

"Where is it?" asked a froggy child, in a low hiss as she peered out into the street. White, knucklebones shone through her papery, green skin.

"The meeting is just down the road, in the safety, Aliya," replied her brother, Dumaire, in an equally low hiss. He licked his thick lips with his forked tongue, and his buggy eyes bulged in the darkness.

The pair hopped on, using their powerful-froggy legs to leap down the street in great bounds.

Above them in the sky, UFOs crisscrossed the night, but the children kept a wary eye on them, as they skulked in the darkness. Curfew was just a reality these days.

Aliya scanned the sky as she hopped, but she jumped too far, and out of nowhere, a garbage can was right in her landing path. She crashed into it, spilling the garbage and metal can on to the sidewalk. A thundering rolling sound bounced off the buildings, which was only halted by a "splosh" as the can fell into the water.

"What did you do?" hissed Dumaire, pulling his sister up. Suspiciously, he looked up. "We've got to hide. Go!"

Two large crafts hummed above in an instant, drawn by the noise and disturbance on an otherwise deserted street.

Search beams slashed down, sweeping the streets, and lighting up the surface of the canal—looking for curfew breakers.

Aliya felt the blood thump in her throat as the beams cut across each area she passed. Sweat dribbled down her back and from her forehead, moistening her already froggy skin.

She had no sense of past or future, there was only this instant, as the beams scoured the streets right in front of her. They were searching for her, and if they found her, they would disintegrate her. She imagined the heat beam descending; and picking her up up into the air, her skin charred and blackened from the heat. ...And then nothing, but ash. She almost squeaked in fear, but she held on.

One beam was very close, almost as if it could sense her fear and was homing in on it. Aliya crept backwards, her rear pressed hard against the wall of a shop. The beam was almost upon her, its edge was skirting her froggy feet. She backed up to the wall, using her sticky hands and feet to clamber up, away from the bright light.

A clatter and clang came from further down the street— the rattling of another garbage can being toppled. There was a curious "Meow", and a ginger tabby cat jumped up onto the overturned garbage can. It looked defiantly at the beam of light, then proceeded to lick its crotch.

Like dogs, the beams shot off after the cat, who fled along the sidewalk away from the froggy children. Aliya came down as Dumaire clambered out from the doorway he had hidden in.

"We've got to move on," he said, grabbing at Aliya's wrist in his shaking hand. They did not hop down the street anymore; instead, they padded silently in the darkness.

At the street's end was a scrap metal warehouse, filled with odds and ends which washed up on the Gyre. The doors were shut, and the windows were boarded over with pro-Moon posters featuring the reanimated face of the Social Justice Hedgehog with his cyborg skull-cap covering half his face.

The froggy children squelched up to its doors, and Dumaire raised his webbed hand and knocked twice, slowly, then a pause, then once, then a pause then three times, quickly.

"Show the sigil," said a voice from the other side, as the door creaked open just a crack.

Dumaire reached into his trouser pocket and brought out the deflated balloon. He placed it to his lips and inflated it to reveal the puckered and drooping face of Abraham Lincoln.

"They have the code, Pixie Peas-Blossom, take the ward off and let them in."

The door creaked open wider.

"Pass, friend," said the sentry, as she stepped out of the doorway. The froggy children squirmed inside, making sure they were not being followed.

The room was bright after the dark of the street, lit by several glowing orbs of white and yellow.

Many peoples gathered in the large warehouse, milling around as if it were some sort of cocktail party. Pixies buzzed annoyingly around at head height, dive-bombing the crowd; often baring their ass-cheeks to them, but sometimes stopping and talking, and making points. The fairy-folk were making sense, sort of, that was always a good sign.

A gigantic refrigeration unit cooled one corner, making it inhabitable for the Snowmen. They loomed menacingly at everyone—yet, people still mingled with them. They talked and chatted and rubbed shoulder to icy shoulder. The snowmen were large and intimidating, and they stank like no one's business, but in the end, they were just people too, it turned out.

The froggy children bumped their way through the crowd. There were people in swathes, some dressed in rags, with the metal collars from the Moon Men still wrapped around their throats —escapees from the recycling plant and nearby garbage mines. The lights were off on their collars, showing them inactive, but the metal itself was too tough to be broken and removed. There were others as well, ordinary people, bakers and butchers, hairdressers and candlestick makers all mingling and talking.

The froggy children eyed the crowd as they passed through it to the front rostrum. To their left were some of the city's velociraptors, eyeing everyone with menace and clicking their toe-claws.

There were heroes among the crowd too. Aliya spotted the bear and his wife the journalist as the pair stood hand in hand, talking to some of the gathered animals. The bear had a large scar down his face, and Aliya remembered the story of the bear fighting to free the journalist from the initial attack.

Aliya had grown up hearing about the heroes. How the journalist continued to produce her underground art, always changing the medium in which she wrote. Sometimes it was tattoos, sometimes words, sometimes flower arranging, sometimes interpretive dance. That changing had been invaluable for the coded messages which had needed to be sent.

The froggy children pushed to the crowd's front. There was a wooden stage which had been set up, rising a few feet off the ground with burning torches placed on either side.

There was a hushing murmur from the crowd as a tall man in a long trench coat stepped on the damp wood stage. His face was grave and weather-worn. His hair was long and unkempt, falling in ragged ringlets passed his ears. He had a short crop of stubble across his face, and beautiful scars slashed across his forehead.

Aliya felt her heart thump faster and her blood pound in her ears. Her skin felt electric in the presence of Abraham Lincoln, guerrilla leader. He held his hands up to ease the crowd's noise.

"My friends," he began, with a smile, "it has been a long and dangerous road to get here, to this moment. We have all changed. We have all seen suffering and seen joy. We have seen unions," he said, indicating the bear and the journalist. "And we have seen death—so, so much death."

Abraham Lincoln's eyes fell to the floor.

"Our friends shall not have died in vain," he said, drawing a deep breath. "We will not allow it. I will not allow it. For too long we were blind, for too long we were stuck in the past, or gazing into the future and not looking at the here and now, and we allowed the monsters in. No more!" he said, raising his fist into the air.

The crowd followed suit; fists raised into the air with defiance.

"Before we were divided," continued Abe. "We didn't acknowledge our fellow citizens. We failed the Snowmen. We failed the pixies. I failed you all. No more!" he raised his fist again, in salute.

The crowd complied.

"Now, we are together, united: human, animal, chewing gum, dinosaur, zombie, pixies and Snowmen. The Moon came when we were divided and when we were distracted by our own petty needs and wants. That was then, and we don't live in the past. We live in the present. Now, we are focused, we are unified, and we are ready."

The crowd smiled, and chucked each other on the shoulders, like old comrades.

"My friends, we have fought, we have bled, and some of us have died. We have done this to throw off the yoke of tyranny. Our freedom was stolen, our liberty taken and smashed. We were forced to flee, forced to hide, forced into servitude at The Moon's hands. No more!" he shouted again.

"We are not OK with this. We are not even slightly OK with this. This is our time, our present. It should be filled with love and laughter and boring normal everyday things. It should be full of grumbling about taxes and filling your boat with gas.

It should be full of 'what's for dinner', and 'what's on the TV'. But it's not, it's full of slavery, and threats, and ugliness. And we have to fight it."

Abe Lincoln took another deep breath. Aliya could see how tired he was. Crows-feet branched from his eyes, and his hair streaked with white strains. Nevertheless, he also looked stern, and steady as a rock.

His hand raised, and he tugged on his newly grown chin-strap beard.

"I'm not going to tell you we can win," he said, and there was a dull murmuring from the crowd. "I won't lie to you like that. We probably can't win. As the bear will tell you, in the long run, no one can win, we will all die one day. But winning doesn't matter. Resisting does. Winning is a future thing, and we shan't focus on that again—that was how the monsters got here. So instead, we focus on the present, on the here and now, on the resisting."

There were whoops and applauses from the crowd. Aliya's hand stung as she clapped.

"I am angry, my friends, angrier than I have ever been. These should not have been our lives, but they are. We are being called upon to make the best we can of them. This is going to be a long, hard, unfun road we have to travel down," said Abe. He huffed loudly and licked his lips. "Do we give in to despair?"

The crowd responded. "No!"

Aliya felt her heart swell.

"Do we go quietly into the night?" Abe asked.

"No!"

Aliya's face set in grim determination.

"Or do we stand? Do we stay united in the face of this new evil? Do we stand shoulder to shoulder with our fellows and say, 'No more'?"

"No more" shouted the crowd.

Aliya throat felt like it would rip open, if she tried to shout as loud as she could.

"Before we were alone. We tried to be separate, concerned only with our own problems—concerned only with our own fate. No more. We stand together. No man makes history on his own. No being is an island. No person can look after themselves totally. We unite, or we die. We stand together, or we pass into darkness. So, we link one hand with our ancestors and another with our unborn children, and we make the chain of civilisation. And we fight, my friends, we fight."

The crowd roared and stumped their feet on the wet wooden floor.

"We fight for our brothers and sisters. We fight for everyone's right to speak and be heard. We fight for the yesterday we remember. And we fight for the future we hope for. But most of all, we fight for this moment, because this is the only moment we have."

They crowed cheered and applauded as Abe finished his speech. Aliya smiled, the first she'd had in a long time. Because they were not alone, they were together. And that was all that mattered, being together and not giving up, and looking at where you stood and understanding it.

The crowd seized the moment.

About Author:

Chris Meekings is a writer from Gloucester.

Several of his works have appeared on Bizarro Central's Flash Fiction Friday. His bizarro novella, "Elephant Vice," was released in 2015 as part of the New Bizarro Authors Series. His novel, "Ravens and Writing Desks," was published in 2016 by Omnium Gatherum. He is a founding member of the British Bizarro Community who recently released the anthology The Bumper Book of British Bizarro, all profits of which go towards the Mermaids Trust.

He is currently 58 weasels in a trench coat, just looking for love.

Hybrid Sequence Media Bibliography

2020
Bring Something Dead
Meat Grinder
From the Belly of the Goat
Mr. Miyagi's Soggy Cereal
Separation: Healing
Rogue
Shrapnel
The Word For Poetry Is Poetry
Catacomb Kittens
Bottomlands

2021
Emotional Time-Lapse
Chicken Lust
A Predisposition for Madness
The Unreliable Narrator
Snailbutter
Tales from the Vinegar Wasteland
Adding to a Map with No Territory
Tomorrow's Gone

2022
Beautifully Broken